INEVITABLE DECEPTIONS 1

The Heart's Journey to Nowhere

By

Sheena Perry

SHEENA PERRY

Copyright

Inevitable Deceptions 1

Copyright © 2017 Sheena Perry

Published by Sheena Perry

Edited by Sheena Perry

ISBN: 0-9986999-0-X
ISBN-13: 978-0-9986999-0-5

INEVITABLE DECEPTIONS 1

The *Tea* on the Author

Sheena Perry is originally from Dallas, TX. She was raised by her teenage single mother, Tonya. Sheena is the oldest of two children. Sheena's mother fell prey to the booming crack cocaine era of the 1980's. Entrusting a close relative with the task of babysitting her two kids, Tonya left for work one day not realizing that the family member would leave them alone and call DCFS.

At tender age of three, Sheena and her brother were removed from the home and placed into separate foster homes. While her brother was placed into a fairly nice foster home, she however suffered unimaginable abuse at the hands of her foster parents. She went days without eating, was fed dog food and she was tied to a chair throughout the day. Her thighs are still branded with the markings from the tight ropes.

Her mother was able to quickly regain custody of both children. However, later the same year she was molested by her mother's fiancé. Immediately reporting the abuse to her mother, the monster was quickly apprehended and served a lengthy stint in prison. Prison did not stop Sheena's molester from issuing out death threats.

He was heavily involved in the drug world and his threats were taken very seriously. Sheena's mom relocated her small family to Columbus, GA. After experiencing such traumatic events, she became extremely shy and withdrawn. She was even mute for two years. The once bubbly outgoing little girl had been replaced by an insecure, self-loathing shell of her former self.

As she became older, Sheena would contemplate suicide numerous times to cope with the unfortunate cards she had been dealt. She had even developed an eating disorder in her mid-teens. Sheena's mother continued to battle with her drug addiction throughout her childhood and into her young adulthood. Sheena has always had a deep passion for reading and writing. Reading has always been her outlet to escape the obstacles that she faced on a daily basis.

She enjoys romance, mystery, horror, autobiographies, thrillers and urban novels. From an early age, Sheena had tutored kids much older than herself. Sheena particularly enjoys writing short stories and poetry. She currently lives in Florissant, MO. Despite her rough beginnings, she was able to conquer all of her hurdles and meet many of her goals.

She was able to purchase her first house at the age of 20. A year later she gave birth to her daughter, Aaliyah. Somehow, she managed to overcome the murder of her daughter's father, who was killed by the police when their daughter was just 4 months old. She is a Registered Nurse. Sheena has a Master's degree in Nursing Education. She is currently in school pursing her Doctorate degree.

She works as a nursing professor at a major university and is the Director of Nursing at a long-term care facility. Sheena is also a licensed foster parent. Having had such a horrific experience during her time in foster care, she wanted to offer a safe home to children in need.

Please stay tuned for **Inevitable Deceptions: The Heart's Journey to Nowhere 3** which is Sheena's third and final installment of the series. She also co-wrote the children's book **I Made You From Scratch: You Are Perfect** with her daughter.

In addition to Inevitable Deceptions: **The Heart's Journey to Nowhere 3**, she is currently working on three other books:

The Whore Next Door: Welcome to Thotville, Do No Harm: License to Kill and ***Help! I Ate Peanuts, Now My Throat's Swelling Up!*** She has also published novels such as ***The Girl Behind The Smile*** by Dornisha Goodrich, ***God Showed Me More Than Heaven*** by K.S. Fisher and ***The Living*** by Frank Washington. Please stay tuned!

I attribute my success to this – I never gave or took any excuse. – Florence Nightingale

Connect with Sheena

Visit her website at www.sheenaperrypublishing.com

Friend her on Facebook at www.facebook.com/sheena.p.rn

Link with her on LinkedIn at
www.linkedin.com/in/sheena-perry-msn-rn-cne-22352486

Follow her on Twitter at www.twitter.com/sheenamperry

Follow her on Instagram at www.instagram.com/sheenamperry

You can also visit her business page at
https://m.facebook.com/SheenaPerryPublishing/

Submissions for all genres are now open. Please submit the first 3-4 chapters of your manuscript for publishing consideration. Allow up to 30 days for a response. Complete contact information including name, address, contact number and email. Use 12 pt. font, double-spaced in manuscript style format. Email manuscripts to submissions@sheenaperrypublishing.com.

We look forward to hearing from you!

Dedication

I'd like to dedicate this book to all of those who have been on the receiving end of abuse. Always know that it is never your fault. You are not alone. Don't be ashamed. Be your own advocate; seek help immediately before it is too late. Do not let your abuser have power over you. Remember that if they've abused you once, chances are that they will strike again.

In loving memory of Michael Calvin Perry, Doris Marie Green, Carolyn Marie White, James Green, Samuel Keita DeBoise and Erin LeighAnna Nabe.

I love and miss you all more than anyone will ever know. Rest in paradise.

~Sheena

Table of Contents

Acknowledgements

To my loving mother, Tonya Perry, I appreciate you for always being my biggest cheerleader. You have always inspired me to challenge myself. You are the strongest person that I know. I love you so much Ma!

To my brother, Rico, we may not always see eye to eye but know that I will always love you to the moon and back. No one can make me laugh the way that you do. You are my best friend.

To my beautiful daughter, Aaliyah, the day that I had you was by far the happiest day of my life. You made me grow up overnight. You are growing into the most amazing young woman that I could ever ask for. I know that your dad is smiling down at you from heaven. I hope that I have always been a positive role model for you and that you realize that you are my biggest motivator. All of my accomplishments were achieved with you in mind. Remember the sky is the limit and that the word *never* is not a part of our vocabulary. I love you baby girl.

To my friends and colleagues that have put up with my endless brainstorms and offered words of encouragement, I thank you for everything. I'd also like to thank my test readers who have given me constructive criticism.

I'd also like to give a special thanks to my readers who have purchased, downloaded and rated my books. You will never know how much your love and support mean to me.

Lastly, I'd like to thank the good Lord above. Thank you for continuing to bless me. Without you, none of this would be possible.

~Sheena

*****WARNING*****

THIS NOVEL CONTAINS STRONG LANGUAGE, BROKEN ENGLISH, SEX, VIOLENCE, AND VULGAR SITUATIONS WHICH MAY BE OFFENSIVE TO SOME READERS.

« Chapter 1 Inevitable »

Present Day "Celeste"

I WAS IN A STATE OF SHOCK as I lay on the filthy cream-colored carpet. I was wide-eyed and tightly clutching my leaking abdomen. The bright red blood that managed to seep between my small fingers was so damn warm...although I was extremely cold and was shivering. My ears were ringing from the deafening shots that were sure to seal my fate.

Who could have predicted that I would have been met with such a dark and vicious ending? I'm not exactly sure how many times I had been struck. I had completely blacked everything out after the first two bullets connected with my flesh. Fortunately for me, my adrenaline level was on a thousand right now, therefore I felt no pain.

I imagine that under normal circumstances my injuries would be excruciatingly painful. Yet I felt absolutely nothing, except cold. I didn't even feel fear. Why should I fear death? Why do any of us fear death? Hell, death is an inevitable part of life.

Aside from paying taxes, death was the only thing guaranteed to any of our asses. No, I was not fearful, but my heart was breaking for my two daughters. My oldest daughter's name is Autumn and my youngest daughter's name is Wintress. I think the origin of their names is quite obvious. Autumn is fifteen and Wintress is eight.

My heart ached for them because although my attacker was oblivious to their presence prior to him fleeing the scene, I knew deep down that they were home hiding somewhere and had most likely heard everything that had transpired. I was not the best mother by a long shot, and I know that I had wronged a lot of people over the years. However, I did not think that bitch named Karma would retaliate in such a brutal way.

Not only did this bitch come back to bite me in the ass, but she bit me on the asshole as well. Deep down I know that I deserved every second of what was happening at this moment. I just could not fathom why my children always had to suffer behind my bullshit. My intuition was confirmed as I saw both of my daughters running at full speed towards me.

Wintress had waterfalls streaming down her red cheeks. Her curly hair was disheveled, and I noticed that she was covered in dust. Snot was threatening to drip onto her upper lip. Her blood shot eyes were etched with worry as she assessed my bullet riddled body. She reached down to touch my blood drenched shirt as I flinched and screamed, "Noooooooo!!!" In a barely audible voice.

She looked at me shocked and inquiringly. I felt terrible. There were so many things that I wanted to elaborate on as to why I did not want her to touch me at that moment. This was just not the time or the place for that.

Autumn wore a blank expression on her face as she called for medical assistance. I wanted to tell her to hang up and not to even bother to try and save me. I knew that I was dying and there wasn't a damn thing even the best paramedic, nurse or doctor could do about it. I had learned long ago that good things rarely happened to me. Making it out of this shabby apartment alive simply was not in the cards.

I refrained from speaking because I did not want to appear selfish in front of my girls. Also, I was just too weak to verbalize my apprehensions. Autumn calmly explained to the dispatcher that I had been shot multiple times. She did not cry, and I knew it was not because she did not love me, but because I had raised her that way. I had been taught that crying was for weak people.

Crying never helped make any situation better. Like an obedient child, she exhibited her poker face. I did not want my girls to cry for me. Although I hated that I had to leave them under these circumstances, I knew that my death was necessary. I had done too much to continue on. My death would potentially save the lives of so many other people. I was slowly dying anyway.

I just hated the fact that the asshole pressed fast forward and decided to take me away from my girls before Autumn's eighteenth birthday. Sadly, that was my only goal in life. Given my dreaded prognosis, I knew better than to plan any long-term goals. I never imagined that I wouldn't even be around to fulfill the short-term goals either. I wanted to live long enough for Autumn to become an adult. I knew that she'd then be able to care for herself and Wintress.

Autumn was one of the strongest people that I'd ever known, even at her age. She was a great big sister as well. There was nothing that she wouldn't do for Wintress. I had witnessed firsthand how much she was willing to sacrifice to ensure that her little sister didn't go without. Sacrifices that I should've been making as the parent. As I stated before, I would never win a Mother of the Year award, but as shitty as I may have been, at least I was better for them than the uncertainties they were now sure to face in the system.

Autumn was well aware that I was sick and probably understood why I was shot down like a rabid dog. She was an extremely bright young woman and I only hoped that she'd turn out so much better than me. I prayed that she would take in all of my past mistakes and learn from them, not mimic nor embrace them. I glanced at both of my young beauties and mouthed the words, "I'm sorry and I love you," over and over again.

I truly hated myself at this moment as I took in what I knew were to be my last images of them. They didn't deserve to be exposed to this shit. It became more difficult to breathe and that caused me to panic internally. I tried my best not to alarm them more so than they already were. I know that I must have been a frightening sight to see. I heard sirens in the background as both of my daughters kissed my forehead and stroked my hair.

I remember Wintress begging me to stay awake and reassuring me that I was going to make it. The last thing I heard Autumn whisper to me was, "I promise I'm going to get him for you momma. I promise!" She hissed.

I weakly shook my head no, at my vengeful daughter. After taking in one last haggard breath, darkness consumed me as EMS began to pound loudly on the door...

« Chapter 2 The Promise »

Present Day "Autumn"

WHILE MY LITTLE SISTER Wintress and I were preparing for bed in the room we shared, I suddenly heard a loud commotion coming from the living room. My mom had finally come home after a week-long hiatus and she obviously was not alone. I heard her admitting to her company that she was HIV positive and that it wasn't *that* bad to live with. Her voice was laced with ice and her nonchalance was unsettling. Somehow, I knew this was not going to end well. I couldn't hear everything that the man said back, but I did hear him call my mother several bitches, a few hoes and one or two muthafuckas.

The man spoke in a whispered tone, so I was unsure of his identity. I assumed that he was whispering because he knew that my mother had children and didn't want us to overhear their conversation. I then heard my mother yell at her guest that no one had forced him to fuck her raw. She told him that he was a grown ass man and it was up to him to strap up. She then proceeded to tell him that he was lucky that she had even threw a little charity pussy his way, because his stroke game was weak as hell. It was then that I heard a loud slap followed by my mother screaming.

She instantly apologized to this guy and stated that she was unaware that she was HIV positive when they first hooked up a year ago. She cried that after finding out; she did not inform him only because she was afraid that she would lose him. She had quickly changed her tune as she looked to the furious mystery guy for some understanding. After hearing this revelation, you'd think that the identity of this mystery man would have been revealed. Unfortunately, I was still clueless. My mom had an extremely friendly pussy...an extremely friendly *sick* pussy. I also noted that she had told this guy a bold-faced lie when she stated that she was recently diagnosed.

My mom was diagnosed with HIV when Wintress was one. That was seven years ago! I remember Wintress being tested for years, thankfully her tests continued to be negative. If I am not mistaken, due to her lack of compliance with her antiviral cocktail coupled with her frequent drug use, she was recently upgraded to full blown AIDS. I had eavesdropped during her last sporadic visit to the doctor. Several doctors had tried to convince her to take better care of herself, but it all fell on deaf ears. Getting high and running the streets were of higher importance to my mother.

Despite knowing that she was living foul as hell, I still loved her. It is amazing the unconditional love that a child has for their parents, no matter how flawed they are. We cannot choose our family members, so I embraced them no matter how shitty they were. The few that I had anyway. Screaming and the knocking over of various objects were heard coming from the living room. As the fighting continued, I looked at Wintress and put my index finger up to my mouth signaling for her little ass to be quiet. I turned off the light in our bedroom and we both hid under the tiny bed we shared.

I know what you're thinking...but we literally had no place else to hide in that little ass room. I used some old stuffed animals in the hopes of obstructing the asshole's view in the event that he waltzed his ass in here looking for us. Out of nowhere I heard a loud popping sound followed by three others. I was not a fool; I instantly knew what that noise represented. I covered Wintress's mouth because I knew that I wanted to scream like crazy, so it was only fair to assume she had to be feeling the same way.

I heard the man yell, "Fuck! Fuck! Bitch, look what your stupid ass made me do! You killed me, so I had to kill you! Fuck!!!"

He must have asked my mom where Wintress and I were, because I heard my mom whisper that we were spending the weekend with our fathers. Yes, that was meant to be plural. We did not have the same dad. Hearing her voice, I couldn't help but to feel joyful that she was still alive. Maybe he hadn't shot her after all.

Her deceptive disclosure was followed by hasty footsteps towards our bedroom door. I heard our door swing open followed by the light being flicked on. I silently thanked God that I had made the bed this morning. Our room was tidy, and our bed was still undisturbed. It did not appear that we had been home today. I heard our bathroom and closet doors being opened. It was then that his bright personalized sneakers came into focus.

I knew exactly who this bastard was! I watched as his large feet stopped beside our bed. My heart rate quickened and began to beat out of my chest. I swore it was so loud that you could hear it. sweat beads formed on my forehead. My grip tightened on Wintress's mouth as my eyes snapped shut. I was bracing myself for him to snatch our asses from under the bed and make Swiss cheese out of us as well. Just as he was about to kneel down and peek under the bed, my mother began to scream for help.

She was still cursing the man out for shooting her as he quickly ran from the room. He then cowardly retreated from our tiny apartment, but not before letting off one more popping sound that instantly silenced my mother. I breathed a bittersweet sigh of relief. I knew her outbursts were done intentionally to distract him from finding us. I was also aware that her heroic action may have sealed her fate.

After waiting a couple of minutes, we felt it was safe to come out of our hiding place. I knew my mom was shot and probably dead at this point. All of her screaming had ceased after we heard that final pop. We slowly walked out of our room and into the entrance of the living room. My sister was crying her heart out and became absolutely hysterical once she spotted our mother on the floor. We both quickly ran over to her and I was shocked when I noticed that she was still alive.

I knew that my mother's wounds were extremely serious. In fact, I knew they were most likely fatal. She had been shot twice in the abdomen, once in the chest and once in the right arm. The last gunshot wound had me ready to pass out. This sick fuck had literally shot my mother in the pussy. Witnessing that shit had my genitalia hurting. She was covered in blood from head to toe. That shit was even oozing from her mouth.

I had never seen that much blood in my entire life, then again, I had never witnessed anything like this before. My mom had a look of shock on her face. We did not have cell phones, but we did have one land line. I was sure that other people had heard the gun shots and had already phoned 911, however in the rare event that they hadn't, I decided to call myself. Deep down I knew they wouldn't be able to save her, especially with her already compromised health.

I watched as my sister innocently attempted to embrace our dying mother only to be stopped. While my sister was too young to understand, I knew exactly why my mother would not allow my sister to touch her. She did not want Wintress to come in contact with her tainted blood. I knew that I would have to explain it all to her one day, but today was not that day. I may seem cold to some because I was not crying and appeared void of any emotions. It was just my way. The truth is, my mom did not like for us to cry...so I never did. I was however crying on the inside.

Strangely in a sick twisted way, I was happy that my mother would no longer have to suffer. She would no longer be in pain, would no longer struggle with her drug addiction and would no longer have to stress out about us. I loved the hell out of her and overlooked all of her many mistakes. Most importantly, I loved her enough to let her go with an understanding in my heart.

I knew she was tired and was only holding on until I was legally able to care for myself and Wintress. She never wanted anyone else to raise us. I stood there and watched as she apologized to the two of us, before life slipped away from her. Before she died, I made a promise to her that her murderer would pay!

« Chapter 3 No Fairytale »

The Past "Celeste"

TRUTHFULLY IF YOU ARE looking for an everlasting, romantic fairytale then you have come to the wrong place. Like most young girls, I dreamed about Prince Charming coming to rescue me from this hell that I know all too well as life. I wanted the white dress, the picket fence, the kids, the dog and an intact hymen on my wedding night. Many outsiders envied the fact that I was raised in a two-parent home, but only if they knew half of the things that transpired behind closed doors.

My name is Celeste Monroe, but everyone calls me Cee Cee for short. I was born October 31st, 1978. I grew up an only child in an extremely strict and religious household in Hazelwood, MO. My mother, Gladys, was an elementary school teacher in the city of St. Louis, Missouri. My father, Lukas or Mr. Monroe, owned and operated several of the local laundromats. Both of my parents worked extremely hard to keep up with appearances. Their disciplinary methods may not have always been the best, but in hindsight I do believe that they had extremely high hopes for me.

I certainly felt the pressure being the only child. I was monitored under a microscope and constantly scrutinized. Very little went unnoticed by my parents. We attended church services three times a week. I was only allowed to wear dresses that came to my knees or below. While my mom did spend a fair amount of money on my clothes, I was never allowed to wear the popular styles that the other teenagers rocked. I was dressed like an expensive old woman. I was never allowed to wear makeup, perfume or fingernail polish aside from clear.

Attendance at the dinner table was mandatory as were prayers prior to meals and at bedtime. Interactions with the opposite sex were nonnegotiable. The only exception to that rule was our next-door neighbor Shawn. I suppose that's because we were practically raised together. I am sure to many, we were the perfect family. We were comparable to the Huxtables even. We led everyone to believe that we lived the ideal middle-class life and appearances were everything to my parents. Boy, did we have all of their asses fooled.

What the outsiders did not see, were typically not visible to the naked eye. The abuse was intolerable. Over the years, my once tolerable father had developed a deep love for alcohol and gambling. He was always a little cool when it came to me. I had never been permitted to call him dad. He demanded that I call him Mr. Monroe. Mr. Monroe never showed me any affection, but he had never raised his hands to me until his alcohol addiction spiraled out of control. He became extremely angry and abusive towards me as well as my mother.

Eventually she joined him and started abusing me as well. She never physically hit me, but she participated in the torture. She contributed greatly to my misery. I suppose it was out of fear. I guess she was hoping that if they became allies then he'd refrain from hitting *her* as often. She was right. I received unfathomable punishments if I brought anything less than an A home on my report cards. I had received beatings with switches, extension cords, hangers, shoes, brushes, fists and any other stray object that my father could reach.

I had been burned as well, but the worst was when my

wrist was broken for forgetting to take out the trash the day before. As bad as this all sounds, the psychological and verbal abuse was so much worse than the physical. I would be deprived of food for days for the most miniscule of things. Last week during my lunch period at school, I opened my lunch sack to discover that my lovely mother had served me a heaping helping of dog food. We didn't even have a fucking dog! Attached I found a lovely little note that read, "Next time you will remember to empty the dishwasher!" I was so disgusted, but more than that I was hungry.

I hadn't been allowed to eat supper the night before. I was too hungry at the moment to even recall why. I blinked back the hot tears that threatened to fall from my eyes. My mom had taught me long ago that crying did not change your circumstances. It didn't lessen the blow of whatever pain you were experiencing.

Besides I needed to conserve what little energy I had left to make it through the remainder of the day. I got up and ran from the school cafeteria, because all of the different aromas were making me lightheaded. I needed fresh air and I needed food as well. I figured that I would not be receiving food anytime soon, so I had to make do with the fresh air for now.

As I sat on a bench outside in deep thought, I felt someone sit next to me. I was feeling so low at that moment that I didn't even bother to look up to see who it was. I recall someone taking me by my shoulders and shaking me while calling my name at the same time. I finally focused on the person next to me.

I was surprised to see that it was Kennedy, the most popular girl in school. Of course, her two shadows, Gia and Layla were standing next to her. They all happened to hate everything about my existence. But I had to admit, they were all very pretty. What on earth could they possibly want with *me*?

After gathering my thoughts, I asked, "What do you want Kennedy?" I figured there was no point in beating around the bush.

I had nothing personal against her, but I knew she thrived on making my life miserable for some reason. Kennedy responded, "I was just checking on you girl, that's all. I saw you sitting over here, and you didn't look well."

I guess I must have really been out of it because I now had a small crowd of nosy onlookers surrounding me.

"I'm okay now. Thanks for checking on me," I genuinely replied.

"Look Celeste, I know we haven't always seen eye to eye. I've been doing some soul searching and I would like it if we could bury the hatchet and become friends. Can we just let bygones be bygones?"

I was speechless. That was all I had ever wanted. We didn't necessarily have to be friends; I just wanted peace at school. I already caught enough hell at home.

"Wow Kennedy, I would love it if we could be cordial with one another. I'm tired of all this drama between us. I'm willing to move on if you are serious about this," I stated.

"Of course, I'm serious. We are getting too old for this same song and dance. I'll even shake on it," she joked while dramatically extending her perfectly manicured hand.

We both burst into a fit of laughter. "Well look Celeste, I noticed that you didn't eat lunch. I saw you run out here and decided to check on you. My mom made lasagna last night and sent me an extra piece. I also have a slice of garlic bread and a can of Pepsi. I've heated it up already. Here, eat it girl," she offered.

I glanced at her, to her shadows and then to the people looking on. As badly as I wanted to turn down her offer, I was starving. My pride had vanished long ago. I hadn't eaten since I ate yesterday's lunch. My stomach growled loudly once she opened the container and the smell of the food reached my nostrils. It smelled heavenly. I graciously thanked her and prayed over the food. I slowly began to eat. I wanted to be a pig and scarf the food down, but I was too embarrassed with everyone still standing near me.

I complimented Kennedy's mothers' culinary skills several times as I continued to eat. As I took my last bite, I noticed that everyone was still standing in their original places, but were now smiling at me. It was strange, but I tried not to think anything of it. Kennedy and I had just squashed our lifelong feud and I didn't want to mess things up by asking her silly questions.

I stood up because our lunch period had ended over fifteen minutes ago. I thanked Kennedy again and told her that I would return her Tupperware bowl after I washed it for her.

She scoffed and cocked her head to the side. "Bitch, did you *really* think that I'd ever want to be friends with your obsolete ass? You are a nobody! You think you're all that because your dad owns his own business and your mother is a schoolteacher. You think your black ass is better than us because your family has money. Just so that we're clear, I hated you when I first met you and I hate your uppity ass now!" Kennedy spat.

I attempted to speak but she quickly stated, "Bitch! Don't interrupt me, I am not finished. You're nobody; therefore, you have nothing to say to me. I just have one question for you Celeste..." I just glared at her without speaking.

She was silent for a few moments before asking, "How does the football team taste you little slut? Luckily for you, only a few of the guys wanted to participate in my cum filled lasagna recipe, but it was enough to serve its intended purpose. I started to add my pussy juice as well, but bitch you will never be worthy of tasting me. So again, how did it tas..."

Before I realized what was happening, I threw a punch to her perfectly sculpted chin. This was followed by me body slamming and showering her face and body with more blows. As I continued the well-deserved assault on Kennedy, I began to have flashbacks of all the torment she had caused me over the years. She had put gum in my hair in elementary school. She had ruined a science project that I had spent a month completing. I receive a D on that project and had gotten my ass royally beaten for it.

Kennedy would tell random guys that I liked them and was willing to put out. She would then give their horny asses my phone number which also led to me receiving beatings at home. She broke into my locker and placed a dead rat in there. You name it, she has done it. This is why I was truly hoping to settle our differences today. After her evil deed today, I now knew that would never happen. I was so hurt and angry that I felt as if I could fuck her up for forever. I wanted to kill her for all of the things she had put me through.

Her face was a bloody mess. I had never been in a fight before and I was surprised by my own strength. I was typically on the receiving end of the ass whoopings at home. I continued to kick her ass. Her shadows knew better than to jump in. I felt invincible in this moment and was convinced that I could have handled all three of them if I needed to. Suddenly, I felt a strong pair of arms wrap me into a bear hug. I couldn't move. Whoever it was had to be powerful. No matter how much I struggled to free myself from their grasp, it was all in vain.

"Calm down Ali! Chill killer," the person chuckled.

"I'm not going to let you go until you calm down. Seriously, you need to chill before the teachers come out here to investigate. Are you trying to get suspended or possibly expelled? You messed her up pretty bad already. What she did to you was dead wrong and I'm sorry she did that to you. I heard about her asking the fellas for sperm samples, but I had no idea that she wanted it for this purpose. She is a sick bitch. In case you're wondering, I did not nut in a cup for her nasty ass."

The more he talked; I subconsciously started to calm down. His voice was soothing and his touch relaxing. He must have noticed too because he finally loosened his grip. My focus returned to Kennedy, who was being helped up by her shadows. She heatedly glanced at me with her one good eye. The other one was swollen completely shut.

She spat, "This isn't over bitch! I have something for you!"

She then limped away with the help of her two friends. They all lived in the same projects. They didn't even live in this school district, so I was unsure how they were permitted to attend my school. The trio appeared to be headed towards the bus stop. I couldn't believe that none of the teachers had heard the commotion and witnessed our fight.

I was thankful because I knew that I'd receive the beating at home that I had just delivered to Kennedy. I felt kind of bad for my actions. I knew violence was never the answer, but I blacked out and could not control myself. I turned around so that I could finally see who had deescalated the situation, but saw no one. The crowd had already disbursed. I was a little disappointed because I wanted to thank him, but there was no point in crying over spilled milk. Hell, I needed to get back to class!

∞

I was sixteen years old and while I had a couple of close friends, I knew better than to discuss our family business. I had made that mistake once, but I vowed I'd never do that dumb shit again. I was beaten and locked in the basement for five days last summer after telling my best friend, Alicia, that I hadn't eaten in three days for not making my bed properly. Her mother, Ms. Trina, had overheard our conversation and promptly confronted my parents over the phone.

They demanded that I came home immediately. I was no fool, I hungrily scarfed down the food that Ms. Trina had prepared before I left. I cannot even begin to tell you what I had eaten, because I had devoured it so fast. If I was going to get my ass kicked, I was going to make the shit worth it. Boy, did I get my ass royally kicked! My parents were manipulative in front of others and calculated in how they abused me. They never ever hit me in my face or my lower arms.

My mom almost had a heart attack when she'd realized that my father had broken my wrist a couple of years ago. She was the one who had coaxed me into telling the emergency room nurse and doctor that I had fallen out of a tree. I suppose it was believable because I had always been a tomboy and often escaped to the treehouse that my dad had built for me back when he at least pretended to love me. I felt so alone in the world and I had no one to vent my frustrations to. Not even my diary was sacred in my house. Yes, I was severely fucked up before for having private thoughts. So, I simply stopped writing them.

It was now fall of 1994. Two months into my junior year of high school, I was standing at my locker joking with my friend

Alicia. I thanked God for her every day. Although I was never able to discuss the drama and abuse that happened at home, it was always a breath of fresh air when I was in her presence. Alicia was far from dumb. She knew that I was being abused, but she never forced me to discuss it. That's one of the many things that I loved about her. The few hours spent with her each day were the only times when I felt some sense of normalcy.

She was an extremely gorgeous girl. Alicia was tall standing at five feet eleven inches. She was biracial, mixed with black and white. She had an even sun kissed complexion. Her seductive almond shaped hazel eyes drew a lot of attention. She had full lips and a slight overbite from sucking her thumb until she reached high school. Most men found her overbite to be extremely sexy. Deep dimples also decorated her cheeks. While she was definitely team itty bitty titty committee, she had ass and hips for days.

She was thick in all the right places. Her waist was nonexistent. What I loved most about Alicia was her confidence. She was beautiful inside and out and she had absolutely no filter. She was one of the most opinionated people that I had ever met. As beautiful as Alicia was, she was never afraid to back up her words with her fists. She did not tolerate disrespect from anyone on any level.

She and her ten-year-old twin sisters, Toni and Tori were being raised by her single mother. Her father was not in the picture and made it well-known that he did not think that Alicia was his. Her father was a high-profile attorney who had an affair on his wife. He had failed to inform Ms. Trina about his primary family when he pursued her.

She fell for him hard and fast. It wasn't until she became pregnant that he revealed his true family dynamic. He did not want any more children and was quite verbal about it. Ms. Trina did not believe in abortions so she said to hell with that bastard. She was determined to raise her daughter all alone. She did take Alicia's father to court just to prove what he already knew. While she acted unaffected, I knew that his public denial had to hurt.

She did raise Alicia alone until she met and married the twins' father, Anthony 'Tony' Simmons. He was a good military man who spoiled her and Alicia rotten. He was killed in the line of duty soon after the twins were born. He left Ms. Trina well off financially. Tony's wise investments coupled with multiple life insurance policies left them not wanting for anything.

Nonetheless, Alicia's mother worked extremely hard as a Registered Nurse to support her and her daughters' needs. She also believed in saving for the rainy days. Alicia and her sisters were spoiled rotten and always wore the latest fashions. Her mother ensured that Alicia's hair and nails were always on point. Now that we were sixteen, Alicia had her driver's license. Her mother would often allow her to borrow her secondary vehicle as long as she was willing to help out by dropping off and picking up the twins from school.

Alicia's access to her mother's car helped me out a lot too. It meant that I could rely on my parents less. I tried to avoid them and their malicious wrath as much as possible. I was happy for my best friend; I only wished that my life could be as happy as hers appeared to be.

I suppose I am attractive as well. I am the color of mocha and have the prettiest skin you have ever seen. Blemish free, if you will. I have lashes so long that they rest on my cheeks whenever I close my eyes. My brown eyes are so intense and mysterious that you could find yourself lost in them. I have high cheekbones that give me an exotic look and the deepest set of dimples. I have beautiful heart shaped lips that cover my straight white teeth. I pride myself on never having a cavity. Lord knows that I probably would have been beaten *and* starved, if I ever did develop one.

I was well-endowed with the body of a fully-grown woman. My double D breasts sat high on my chest. My ass and hips gave Serena Williams a run for her money. However, I was considered what people call 'slim thick'. I'm sure that was primarily due to food being withheld so often. I only stood at five feet two inches, so I was always straining my neck to look up at my best friend. Especially on the days when she decided to wear six-inch stilettos.

One of the things that set Alicia and I apart the most was the fact that she dressed with lots of sex appeal. I on the other hand was forced to wear my Little House on the Prairie dresses. My hair was long and healthy, and it reached the middle of my back, however, I usually kept it in a basic ponytail. One thing I was thankful for was the fact that my mother hadn't allowed me to damage my hair with chemicals or weaves.

Although, in hindsight, Alicia and I were equally attractive, I felt inferior and ugly standing next to her in my ordinary clothes. Sometimes I would sneak and wear some of her outfits to school and then change prior to returning home. I had an interview last week at a clothing store in the mall called Divas R Us and I was hoping for a return call.

If I landed the job, I would be able to build my wardrobe up in no time. I would also have extra cash to buy my own food whenever my parents got a hair up their asses and decided to withhold food. I would then be able to start saving for a car. I was surprised when my dad agreed to my interest in finding a job. The job paid six dollars an hour and as far as I was concerned, I was about to be a rich bitch!

« Chapter 4 Upgrade Me »

The Past "Celeste"

AFTER TWO MORE AGONIZING days of waiting, I finally got the call that I had been waiting for. I was scheduled to start orientation the next day. The last cashier had quit abruptly, and they needed coverage immediately. My first day of work was great. All of my new coworkers were very friendly and helpful. My new supervisor was an extremely nice and helpful man named Joe. He appeared to be in his mid to late twenties. He was quite handsome for an older guy. He bore an uncanny resemblance to the actor Lance Gross.

I quickly noticed that he wore a wedding band and thought his wife was pretty lucky to have such a nice husband. He had kind eyes and a bright white smile. He was brown skin and wore his hair in a low-cut fade. He was well over six feet tall, but I never felt threatened. He was patient with me and never made me feel like an idiot whenever I asked questions or made mistakes. He was also willing to work around my school schedule which was a huge bonus.

I was happy to discover that employees received forty percent off all of the merchandise. I smiled as I daydreamed about all the beautiful new outfits I'd soon be rocking to school.

"Celeste, did you hear what I asked you?" Joe asked.

"I am so sorry Joe. No, I didn't, my brain is going into overdrive right now. There is so much to learn. Can you please repeat the question?" I half lied.

"I asked if you wanted to take your lunch break now?" He repeated.

"Sure, I am starting to get a little hungry," I replied rubbing my flat stomach.

I walked to the food court and purchased my meal with some of the money that Ms. Trina had given me. She had vowed to give me a weekly allowance just as she did with her own kids after learning about what Kennedy had done to me. I had used some of the money to buy various snacks. I hid them in my school locker and in my bedroom closet for those inevitable rainy days.

The next couple of weeks flew by and I had finally received my first paycheck. I was so ecstatic. I finally had something with my name on it and it belonged to me. If I didn't need the money so badly, I would've framed it. Ms. Trina had taken me to open my first savings account. I tried to repay her some of the money that she'd given me, but she dismissively waved me off.

"Cee Cee, what I do for you never requires repayment. I still plan to give you your weekly allowance regardless of your job. I should've initiated giving you an allowance a long time ago, but I didn't want to step on your parent's toes. I'm not blind baby. I know things aren't okay at home. I don't question you about it because I try to respect the black parent code of 'what goes on in my house, stays in my house.' I do not want to cause more problems for you. Please know that if things ever become more than you can bear, I will hotline their asses.

I would then fight them tooth and nail for custody of you. Just say the word Cee Cee. Never forget that you are always welcome to stay over here for as long as they allow you to. I just want you to continue to do well in school and save the majority of your money. I know you will probably blow your first few checks on clothes and shoes, but then I want you to start saving. That's how you can repay me sweetie," she replied while giving me a tight hug.

I was so touched by her loving words that I almost allowed a tear to roll down my cheek, but I thought better of it. I thanked Ms. Trina for always being there for me. I loved and appreciated her so much. Why couldn't she be my mother?

As predicted, I blew most of my newly acquired wealth on clothes and shoes. While the clothes that I had purchased were not high end, you couldn't tell the difference once they hugged my curvy frame. My seventeenth birthday was tomorrow, and Alicia had convinced me to get my hair professionally straightened into a wrap.

I wanted my hair to be styled in a more daring style, but I knew my parents would never go for it. In the end, I loved the results. My hair had never looked so pretty and full of body. Alicia kept her hair cut to about shoulder length. She opted for a layered bob with blonde streaks. We both looked hot! Alicia had talked my parents into allowing me to stay over her house tomorrow night for my birthday after spending the day with them.

The day of my seventeenth birthday was much like the others. Now that I was getting older, the physical abuse had lessened in frequency, but the verbal and psychological abuse was always lying just below the surface. My mom had made breakfast and was surprisingly nice. I suppose it wasn't all that surprising. She was always good to me in the absence of Mr. Monroe.

She looked incredibly sad for some reason as if she had a lot on her mind. She and I didn't have the kind of relationship to where I felt comfortable asking if she were okay. For all I knew, she probably would've had Mr. Monroe beat my ass for not 'staying in a child's place.' I liked her much better without my dad around. Things almost felt normal. Almost.

The two of them together was a toxic combination. My father had to work all day, so luckily for me I probably wouldn't see him at all prior to me leaving. My mom had baked my favorite Lemon cake and we surprisingly had a good time reminiscing about the past. She also shared some hilarious stories about her students.

Finally, at five Alicia arrived to pick me up. Alicia was always quiet whenever she came into my house. It was painful watching how forced her interaction with my parents was. It was nothing like the relationship that I shared with Ms. Trina. I felt as if I could talk to her about almost anything. She brought that out of you. I grabbed my overnight bag and waved goodbye to my mother.

Alicia's sneaky ass had a surprise for me. We were going to a house party in North St. Louis off of Natural Bridge road tonight instead of just hanging out at her house. I was nervous because I had never been to a party full of unsupervised teenagers before. I had never been to this area before either. I had often heard of all the crimes that took place out here. Sensing my apprehension, Alicia grabbed my hand and assured me we'd be together the entire time.

She stated that we were some bad bitches and that all the men were going to be riding our asses. I think her attempt to help me relax made me even more nervous. I didn't feel that I fit in with that crowd and didn't want to be judged. Plus, I feared my parents would find out that I had snuck to a party. I didn't know who was going to be present and I had no clue if they knew my parents. My mom had probably taught many of them in elementary school, I was sure of it.

Alicia left her bedroom and quickly came back with two glasses of wine. We had snuck into Ms. Trina's alcohol more times than I could count over the years. I could tell that Alicia was trying another approach to calm my nerves. She had already applied her makeup and her face was beat for the Gods. She was now putting on my face. She had opted to wear a skintight black backless jumpsuit. It was extremely snug and made her ass look even fatter. She selected some red six-inch stilettos and a red clutch to match.

Her flawless makeup made a bold statement. Her full lips were blood red while she'd given her almond shaped eyes the smoke eye look. My best friend was fire! Ms. Trina had purchased my birthday outfit for me. God bless her! It was a white form fitting dress. The neckline plunged dangerously low and the back of the dress was nonexistent as well. The material covered just above my round ass.

This dress was definitely not designed for the saggy breasted women. I thanked God for my perky girls tonight. I decided to rock some 4-inch white heels with straps that wrapped around my chocolate calves. For some reason, I loved wearing white. It complimented my mocha complexion well. I requested natural looking makeup. She applied soft pink eye shadow and lipstick. We were a sight to see.

« Chapter 5 Happy Birthday »

The Past "Celeste"

FROM THE CAR, WE could tell that this party was going to be lit! The wine had helped loosen me up a little bit, but I was still a bundle of nerves. I had never looked or dressed like this before. I had never felt this beautiful in my entire life. As we got out of the car and walked toward the front entrance, all eyes were on us as Alicia had predicted. All we needed was the red carpet laid out in front of us. I was scared because some of the cat calls and whistles were a little aggressive.

Alicia just ate the attention we were receiving up, while I on the other hand wanted to disappear into thin air. One guy even grabbed my hand and rubbed it on his crotch as we were climbing the stairs.

Alicia quickly ended that shit. She got in his face and yelled, "Trey, why is your old ass even at this party? You know your ugly ass is too old to be preying on high school girls. Touch my fucking sister again and see if I don't fuck your nasty ass up and tell your baby momma what you're out here doing!"

"Damn, okay shorty, I didn't know this was your fam. I didn't mean no disrespect. I've never seen her before and just thought she was fine as hell," he softly replied.

"My nigga, I don't want to hear that bullshit you're spitting right now. I don't care who walked up on this porch, you have no right to be touching them or making them touch your little ass dick! Do not let that shit happen again or we will have some serious problems!" She spat as she roughly mushed him in his forehead and left his retarded ass standing there dumbfounded.

I loved this about her. She gave no fucks! The party was packed from wall to wall. I saw a lot of people from our school and some I didn't recognize. The guys played it cool for the most part while the girls were on the dance floor grinding and damn near fucking with clothes on. A lot of the top 90's songs blared in the background. Some of the guys were looking and smelling delicious. I was so excited, yet I felt out of my element. Alicia was dancing and letting loose, yet I had never danced in front of other people before. I was way too shy for that.

A few guys had asked us to dance and while I politely turned each of them down, Alicia danced with a few until she spotted her boyfriend Mike. Mike was a senior and he was also captain of the football and basketball teams. He was very handsome and complimented my friend well. He had dreads down his back. He was caramel complexioned and had dreamy bedroom eyes. He was about six foot four and weighed two hundred and twenty pounds of solid muscle. With Alicia's stilettos, they were nearly eye to eye.

Mike was Alicia's first love...first everything really. I remember the both of us crying after she'd lost her virginity because Mike had taken a week to call her. He explained that his family had to go out of town because his grandfather had passed away unexpectedly. She'd quickly forgiven him, and all was well after that. I'm not sure why, but I have always gotten this weird vibe from him. He's been good to my friend ever since his little disappearing act. So, I overlooked it. That was over a year ago and they were now the hottest couple at school.

As I was sitting on a couch watching everyone have a good time, I was approached by the most handsome guy I had ever seen. Well, I had seen him before around school, but I didn't think he had ever noticed me before. I bet his sexy ass didn't even know my name. Maybe he thought I was someone else tonight because I did look extremely different.

"What's up Ali, you look...you look so different. I mean you look finer than a muthafucka! Damn! I had no idea that you were hiding that beautiful body underneath all those baggy ass dresses. Celeste, you look better than all these bitches in here tonight," Eli exclaimed with confidence.

His eyes danced all over my body before finally landing on my face. So, he was the guy who had calmed me down that day at school. His voice was unforgettable. At this point I was extremely embarrassed and not sure if I should have been flattered or offended. I went with the latter.

"Is that what you consider a compliment? If so, take that bullshit somewhere else. What ever happened to men being chivalrous? Where is the respect? I have boys whistling, yelling and making me grab their little shriveled ass dicks instead of approaching me like a lady. Now you are over here fucking me with your eyes and referring to women as bitches? Get the hell out of here with that shit. With your no game having ass! Take those compliments and shove them up your ass!" I barked.

After snapping on Eli, I was secretly afraid that he was about to fuck me up. I don't know where that courage came from. He was breathing heavily, and his nostrils were flared. He had a wild look in his eyes as he looked around at everyone who had overheard our exchange. I slammed my eyes shut and braced myself for a blow. I was used to getting hurt.

Moments passed and I slowly opened my right eye. I was surprised because he hadn't hit me yet. Out of nowhere, he flashed this huge smile, showcasing his thirty-two pearly whites. I was taken back by his bipolar ass display. I wasn't sure what to expect, yet I was fascinated by his sexy ass. I guess he is what you would consider a rugged pretty boy. I typically found dark skinned guys more attractive, but even Stevie Wonder could see that this boy was gorgeous.

Eli looked a lot like Shemar Moore, but with an edgier look and disposition. He was about six foot two inches. He had a slim, muscular frame and I knew he was active in multiple sports at school. He had a sleeve of tattoos covering his left arm and what impressed me the most about him was the fact that he did not sag.

He knew how to properly dress and made sure that his ass was not hanging out like most of the other guys our age. I could tell he smoked weed. He was most likely high now because his lips were slightly darker than their natural color. Plus, his eyes were sitting low and were slightly reddened.

As I stood up and began to walk away, he grabbed my hand and kissed it. He then asked if we could start over. He asked if I could walk outside with him where the music wasn't so loud. I was apprehensive and feared that he may have only had a change of heart so that he could kick my ass for snapping on and embarrassing him in front of everyone.

As if he read my mind, Eli quickly reassured me that he was not going to hurt me and that he was sorry for coming at me the way he had. He acknowledged that he was aware that my parents did not play and didn't want them coming after him.

I reluctantly followed Eli to the front porch where I was again met by the unfortunate sight of Trey's nasty ass. I had my back turned towards Trey, however I could feel his lust filled eyes burning a hole through me. Eli quickly apologized again and explained that most women took what he had said earlier as a compliment.

"I've had my eyes on you since you and Alicia came into the party. Honestly, I always thought you were beautiful, but I know your parents don't play when it comes to you. I know they'd never approve of a bad boy like me dating their princess. My intentions weren't to disrespect you in any way. To be completely honest with you, I was just nervous and didn't know how to approach you. You had a nigga tongue tied for real shorty. That shit never happens, I *always* have something to say," he explained with a seductive smile.

I avoided eye contact and looked down at my feet. I was nervous and didn't know what to say. He smelled so good and I did not want to say the wrong thing. I was not used to conversing with the opposite sex...especially one that looked like Eli.

He reached over and lifted my chin and asked, "Why are you looking down? Do you not realize how truly beautiful you are? I don't ever want you looking down. That's ugly chick behavior and ugly you most certainly are not. You hear me, Ali?" I gave him a weak smile and nodded my head. I was kind of feeling my new nickname.

"What are you doing at this party anyway? No offense, but I didn't think you were allowed to come to functions like this?" He inquired.

I smiled because I never thought Eli had noticed me before. After all, he was a senior. To my pleasant surprise, he had observed quite a few things about me as well as my life.

"Today is my birthday and Alicia decided to bring me here...well sneak me here. My parents would literally kill me if they knew my whereabouts at this moment," I stated seriously.

"No shit? Happy birthday beautiful! I have to get you something special," Eli shouted firmly embracing me.

I swiftly shook my head and stated that wasn't necessary. He simply smiled and changed the subject. We begin to tell each other about ourselves. I learned that Eli had a fourteen-year-old sister named Malia and an eleven-year-old brother named Daniel. I knew Malia because she went to our school, but I didn't know that she was Eli's sister. Now that I knew, I could see a strong resemblance. The three of them were raised by his paternal grandmother.

Their father was murdered during a drug deal gone wrong and his mother had mysteriously disappeared that same night. I noticed his jaw clench as he spoke about his mother. He never elaborated. I wasn't sure if he thought she had participated in the murder of his father or was also a victim herself. He hated to see his grandmother struggle to support the three siblings with her fixed income, so he resorted to selling drugs.

While I did not agree with him selling drugs, I completely understood why he felt he needed to. His expression was void of any emotion as he told me about his upbringing. His eyes were cold, and his fists were tightly balled up. My heart ached for my new friend. I wished I could take all his pain away.

For some strange reason, I felt comfortable enough to confide in Eli about the neglect and abuse that was going on at home. I prayed that he wouldn't betray me and start spreading my business around the school. I had a lot to lose if this ever got around. I didn't get that gossiping vibe from him. He seemed like a private and discreet person. Trustworthy even. I felt that I could talk to him about any and everything.

He looked furious upon hearing about the beatings and torment I'd encountered over the years. I had to calm him down because he wanted to kick my parents' asses on sight. I told him that I only had a year until my eighteenth birthday, and I would finally be free of them both. I had always received excellent grades and I was hopeful that I'd receive a full academic scholarship. I planned to attend a university as far away from them as possible. I told him that I had just started working at Divas R Us in the mall and would be saving my money.

I wrote down his number, but not before I explained my phone restrictions. He was brought up to speed on the times that I could and couldn't talk. I also had to memorize his number because I didn't want to risk my overbearing, snooping parents finding his number written down.

We hugged and he again wished me a happy birthday before giving me a bundle of one hundred-dollar bills. Before I could decline the money, he quickly turned and walked away. I quickly rejoined the party eager to tell my best friend about my unexpected encounter with sexy Eli.

« Chapter 6 The Bet »

The Past "Eli"

I WAS CHILLING WITH MY boys in this little house party in the hood. It was definitely popping tonight and was comprised of a few possible bed warmers twerking about. I had a nice little buzz from the kush I had smoked and the bump of coke I had snorted right before hitting this little spot up.

Don't get any presumptuous ideas in your judgmental little heads. I am not a coke head, but the shit does help keep a nigga awake and alert. I work long hours monitoring my workers and trap houses. I have a lot riding on me being on point at all times. I'm feeding the hood, so to speak. I am a God to some out here in these streets.

As I was about ready to step up to this thick redbone, I noticed someone who was completely out of place in my peripheral vision. I thought my eyes were playing tricks on me...or maybe I was higher than I thought. I rubbed my eyes twice and then squinted. I'll be damned if I didn't see Celeste's bible thumping little ass in here. How in the fuck did she get away from her psychotic ass, cock blocking parents? She had always been a naturally beautiful girl, but tonight she was sexy as hell.

She looked so fuckable. I had always wondered what curves she had hidden under those big ass old lady dresses. I was certainly not disappointed. Her tits were sitting up perfectly without the assistance of a bra. She has those *independent titties.* Her ass was so thick, and I'd bet my last dollar her shit was soft as fuck. I felt my dick twitch in my pants just looking at her juicy ass as she found a seat on a couch. I found myself discreetly readjusting my dick in my pants. Oh, how I wish I was that couch cushion right about now. Shorty was flawless and I knew somehow, I needed to find a way to sample that pussy.

She looked out of place and was not dancing like most of the other women. I felt like a stalker as I continued to monitor her movements and slowly sipped on some spiked punch. I peeped several lame ass fuck boys proposition her for a dance and her phone number. She politely smiled and dismissed them all. I liked that about her. While all these other thirsty broads...no scratch that. While all these dehydrated bitches were in here trying to hook their next come up, Celeste couldn't have cared less about that life. Celeste was not on a captain save a hoe mission. She was different.

The rational part of me knew that she was too good for me and I didn't deserve her. The selfish part of me knew that I had to get at her ass sooner than later. She had blossomed overnight, and I knew these niggas were dying to cuff her little ass. My partner in crime named Country noticed me watching little momma and called me out on that shit.

"Aye nigga, I'm gonna need yo peeping Tom lookin ass to take a picture. You've been staring at shorty for hella long...I'm surprised she hasn't taken out a restraining order against yo ass yet!" Country joked prompting the rest of our little group to break out into a fit of laughter.

"Come on now, it ain't even like that. I'm not checking for her like that. I like my hoes easy. I bet she is still a virgin and I don't have time to talk no bitch out of any new pussy. I just can't believe her crazy ass parents finally decided to cut the umbilical cord. What the fuck is she doing in here yo?" I asked no one in particular.

"In all the years I've known you, I have never known you not to step up to a challenge. I think yo ass is frontin like you don't want to smash shorty because you know you can't get close to that pussy. I bet her pops put a chastity belt on her ass and threw away the key," Country rebutted.

"My nigga, who the fuck is you talking to? It is me! Eli! You know me better than that. I'd have her ass calling me daddy in a week! But my point is, why invest a week in these hoes when you can stick and move in a day?" I seriously questioned.

Country replied, "Okay Lil Shemar looking ass muthafucka. Here's the deal. I will bet yo ass a G that you can't get your dick wet by *her* pussy within the next week. Actually, you know what, since I'm in a generous mood I will give yo yella ass two weeks to bust that cherry. Also, I'm gonna need proof before I cash out. Record that shit or something. Is that enough of an incentive?" Country challenged.

I'm not a conceited nigga or nothing, but I knew that most women would find a muthafucka like me a good catch. I usually didn't have to put in much, if any effort to get my dick wet. My pretty boy looks coupled with my thugged out swag, most certainly had its advantages in the pussy department. I was a little hesitant to accept Country's deal because I really didn't feel like chasing shorty like that. She was different and I knew that in this two-week timeframe I was going to have to court her ass, play a sucker and make her fall for me.

Hell, I might even have to shed a few tears and say the "L" word to appease her ass. I knew she wasn't going to hand over the pussy unless she thought she loved a nigga. Normally I didn't care about a bitch or her feelings, but I knew that she had already been through a lot. The streets talk and I knew her parents were on some bullshit. I didn't want to hurt her after I popped her cherry, but I damn sure wasn't about to turn down easy money. I wasn't hurting for money or anything, but I was a greedy bastard. Money talks and as you all know, bullshit walks.

I accepted that fool's bet and we shook on it. I decided that I would make my move tonight since there was no telling when I would be able to get this close to her again without her parents' present. I headed over in her direction as everyone slow grinded to one of R. Kelly's many baby making songs.

She appeared shocked to see me standing in front of her. She was even more beautiful up close. I cannot recall ever being this close to her, aside from the day of the fight. She smelled edible as hell. After initiating the conversation and shorty going off on me, I will admit that I almost beat the fuck out of her.

If you can talk big shit, then you could get the fuck slapped out of your ass. I was complimenting the bitch, but she felt I was being disrespectful. Usually I don't even compliment these hoes outside of saying they have a fat ass or dick sucking lips. Hell, she should've been happy. I tell ya, these bitches were ungrateful as fuck these days! Maybe my approach was not the greatest, but for the first time in a longtime a nigga was nervous as fuck.

I don't know what it was about Celeste, but I had to get it together. After conversing for a minute, I asked her to come outside so that we could talk without having to yell over the music. She looked scared, but I assured her that she was safe with me. I would let her little disrespectful rant slide for now, only because I had a mission to accomplish. I would make that pussy pay later for her slick ass mouth. Next time she wouldn't be so lucky.

After relocating to the porch, I noticed Trey's pedophile ass grilling shorty. I didn't address his wandering eyes then because I didn't want to scare Celeste off in the event a fight was to occur. You better believe he would be dealt with at a later time. For all he knew, she was my bitch. You don't look at another niggas bitch the way he was looking at Celeste. That was pure disrespect towards me. I found that talking to Celeste was almost therapeutic. I felt comfortable discussing my past with her. She was a great listener and was nonjudgmental.

I was ready to murk both of her shitty ass parents for some of the shit she told me about them. I couldn't believe that she had to live through that on a daily basis. I immediately wanted to protect her, especially from her father. I had heard about his punk ass on the streets. For me, I had to get at him on a personal level anyway. He had just given me another reason to leave his ass stanking in an alley.

After finding out it was her birthday, I knew that I had to do something special in order to score some brownie points with her. I highly doubted that she had ever had a boyfriend before so hopefully she was easily impressed. It was getting late and I needed to go and check on a couple of my trap houses. Before I left, I made sure we exchanged phone numbers. I felt like I was dealing with a little ass girl after she rattled off a bunch of 'phone rules'.

It was cool though, I planned on playing my role and being patient. Looking at her full, pink painted lips had me wishing they were wrapped around my meaty nine-inch dick. I was definitely going to have to bust down someone's throat tonight. Shaking those thoughts out of my head, I dug into my pocket and retrieved the stack of c-notes that I always carried around for emergencies. I peeled off twelve c notes and handed them to shorty before disappearing into the darkness...

« Chapter 7 Deadbeat »

Present Day "Autumn"

EVERYTHING WAS HAPPENING so quickly. I was in a daze as I watched police officers, homicide detectives, paramedics, crime scene investigators and God only knows who else scrambling about the cramped apartment. I pinched myself numerous times to ensure that I were awake and that this wasn't just some fucked up nightmare. My mom had been pronounced dead at the scene and her body was still uncovered. Pictures were being taken of both her and of the crime scene. I don't know which of those assholes referred to my mother as "the body" but it unnerved me to the point that I snapped.

Up until that point I was stoic and emotionally detached from the commotion surrounding me. Something about my mother being reduced to just a body pissed me the fuck off.

All I remember was screaming, "Do you bastards not have any fucking respect for my mother?! She is not "the body" her fucking name is Celeste Monroe! Refer to her as a damn body again and see if I don't fuck each and every one of you assholes in here up! How many pictures do you cunts need? Hurry the fuck up and cover my mother! Get her off of that damn floor you useless assholes! You couldn't even save her life, why did I even bother calling you bitches???!!!" That's my last recollection before total darkness consumed me.

Apparently, in the mist of my psychotic break, I had also

destroyed the apartment. I had to be restrained and received a combination dose of Haldol and Ativan straight in my ass. I'm sure it probably didn't hurt at the time, but now my right ass cheek was killing me! I felt terrible. I guess my actions led everyone to believe that I was crazy. They put my black ass on an adolescent psychiatric unit. I didn't deserve this shit. Wasn't I suffering enough? They were treating me like a prisoner because I was in mourning and had grieved the only way I knew how.

I was even more pissed after finding out that Wintress was placed with a foster family. I was distraught that she had to deal with this entire traumatic ordeal alone. I had no idea how to get in touch with my sister. My assigned nurse was nice enough. She was this kind, soft spoken nurse named Briana.

She went over the unit's rules and regulations. She informed me that even if I did locate my sister, due to the strict age restrictions, I wouldn't be able to converse with her over the phone or have her come up for visits. I had never felt so alone in my entire life. Even when my mom wasn't there in the past, I always had Wintress.

My heart ached and longed to be reunited with my baby sister. I prayed that whatever family she was placed with was kind to her. I had so much anger inside of me at that moment. I was disappointed at myself for reacting poorly to my mother's death and ending up in this shit hole. Now my sister was out there living with people who did not love or know her. She was probably with some fat, lazy, evil bitch who was only a foster parent for the money.

I was infuriated with the coward who had taken my mother away from us prematurely. I was even angrier envisioning my mother's cold lifeless body lying on a steel slab in a medical examiner's office. How could she leave us in this predicament? She always promised me that she would live at least long enough to celebrate my eighteenth birthday. I foolishly believed her. In hindsight, I now realized that we were both fools.

She was a fool for making such a ridiculous promise and I was the gullible idiot who believed her lying ass. Lastly, I loathed the fucker who infected my mother with the virus. After her HIV diagnosis, the mother I once knew and loved slowly disappeared. Her entire personality had changed, and it changed overnight. She always seemed to be in a dark place. Her circle of friends went from wholesome people to an unsavory crowd. She'd disappear for a day or two in the beginning, but eventually she'd leave for weeks at a time.

Raising Wintress wasn't always easy, however it came naturally. The few people who knew our circumstances always commended me for taking such great care of my sister. I simply called it instinct. I had been caring for my sister for so long that I didn't know that it wasn't my duty, but instead my mother's.

My mother became an irresponsible teenager and I transitioned into the parent. Thankfully our bills were super cheap due to section 8 housing and our utilities being all inclusive. Since my mother's only income was her disability check and food stamps, our household bills equaled less than three-hundred and fifty dollars.

My mom's disability check was a measly five-hundred and thirty-five dollars per month. With the two-hundred dollars we received in food stamps, I had learned how to get creative. My mom was at least a considerate addict. She never used her disability check or the food stamps to support her habit.

She always allowed me to have the money so that I could take care of the house. She financed her habit by selling her infected pussy to any poor perv willing to buy it and whatever child support she received from my dad. She wasn't all bad. If there was anything extra me or Wintress needed financially, she always made it happen.

∞

We didn't have any family, well, except for my dad. Although he really didn't step up to the plate often, I had really hoped that he would be able to help Wintress and me out now, just this once. At least until I was able to obtain employment after I turned sixteen in two months. Then I figured maybe he could get the two of us a small apartment in his name. Or maybe we could live with him as roommates and I would pay him rent for the both of us. I was willing to do and say anything to get out of this loony ass hospital and avoid my own foreseeable foster home placement once I was discharged.

These other kids in this place were truly certifiable. I just had one bad day and I was on lockdown with these crazy ass bastards. After one of our mandatory groups, I had asked Briana if I could call my dad. She dialed the number for me and handed me the receiver after she verified his identity. After we both handled our pleasantries I got right down to business.

"Dad, my mommy is gone. She was murdered yesterday. I messed up and cursed out the cops. I broke some things in the apartment because they were disrespecting her body. They put me in this crazy hospital and put Wintress in some foster home. I am so worried about her. I don't know what to do or who else to turn to. We literally have no one to talk to. I don't even know who fathered Wintress. As you should know, I will be turning sixteen in two months and then I will be able to legally work.

I do not mean to impose or disrupt your life in anyway,

but can Wintress and I please come and live with you? The nurse said that once I'm discharged from this crazy hospital that I will be going to a foster home too. Once I get a job, I can pay you rent, or you can rent me an apartment in your name, and I will keep up with the rent. We really will not be a problem, I swear it. I know this is a lot, but I have no place else to turn," I spewed my plea so fast that I do not recall taking a breath until I was done talking. Hell, I was desperate!

I finally drew in a deep breath. My heart rate was at least two-hundred beats per minute. My palms were sweaty, and I had suddenly developed the bubble guts. I needed to shit badly, but that had to wait until my phone call had concluded. I was a bundle of nerves and it was amplified by his silence. I grew fearful that the phone call had dropped, and he hadn't heard anything that I had said.

I weakly called out, "Dad?"

After a moment, he cleared his throat and said, "I'm here Autumn."

I whispered, "I was afraid that I had lost you. You were so quiet."

My dad said, "No, it is all just a lot to process. I heard about what happened to your mother on the news. I am so sorry about your loss baby girl. I know you loved your mother a lot. I'm sorry about what is happening to you and Wintress. No child deserves to go through what you two are dealing with right now. Some adults aren't psychologically strong or mature enough to handle your situation. Autumn you are a strong, bright young lady. I have no doubt that you can weather any storm that brews your way.

I've been meaning to tell you that you have a new little

sister. She is three months old and her name is Justice. You also have a new stepmom, Janet. We got eloped last year once we found out that she was pregnant with Justice. The social workers have already called me about the two of you potentially coming here to live with my family.

I've discussed the entire situation with Janet and frankly she is not comfortable with the idea of the two of you being around Justice. After she was informed about your outburst, she fears that you and Wintress may have some unresolved aggression that needs to be treated. Now please try to understand where I'm coming from. You are my daughter and I love you dearly, but I have to do what is best for my family. I am fond of little Wintress too.

If I allowed the two of you to come here, that would cause unwarranted chaos within my household. It would be illegal for me to rent an apartment in my name for minors to occupy. I wouldn't be able to sleep at night knowing that you two didn't have any form of adult supervision. I am just not comfortable with that notion. I know you may not understand my reasons for saying no now, but once you become a parent you will understand.

Again, I know this is probably the most difficult experience you've ever encountered; however, my decision is final. I was assured by the social workers that they would do everything in their power to place you with Wintress, however, it is not a guarantee. You will probably be more difficult to place due to your advanced age. Baby girl, no matter where you are, I will visit you as often as I can. Maybe you will even be able to meet Justice, if Janet is okay with it. Please don't hate me for my decision."

Throughout his recited little speech, I had stolen

occasional glances at my nurse, Briana. She had the most sympathetic look in her eyes. Her looks of pity confirmed that the social workers had already reported to her that my deadbeat ass sperm donor didn't want my sister and I to come and live with him. I know it wasn't Briana's fault and I'm also sure that she was not authorized to divulge that information to me. However, I wish she would've told me his decision before I called this piece of shit and embarrassed myself.

There is nothing more humiliating than humbling yourself and laying all of your cards on the table just to be turned away in your time of need. Time of crisis. I initially contemplated breaking down and begging. However, I would never in a million years give this coward the satisfaction of hearing me cry or beg. I blinked back all of my budding tears. My next reaction was to become livid and curse his pussy whipped ass out and tear this place apart.

How could this spineless prick allow his wife to dictate his relationship with his firstborn? For some reason, I thought better of all of those unsavory reactions. I knew crying and getting angry wouldn't help a damn thing. Knowing that my sister and I truly had no one in this world of over six billion inhabitants hurt me to the core. Knowing that I had failed my sister was enough to make me not want to live any longer. As my sperm donor continued to flap his pathetic jaws, I distastefully looked at the receiver in disgust.

I replied, "Micah, I want to thank you for absolutely nothing. I'd like to wish you and *your family* the very best. Congratulations on the *new baby* as well as the *new wife*. I hope that they never have to find out what it feels like to become the *old*. Visits will not be necessary or welcome. You're right about one thing; my mom raised me to be an incredibly strong woman. Please know that I will be okay. Goodbye, Deadbeat!" I heard him call out my name as I roughly concluded the phone call.

« Chapter 8 Ms. Kitty »

The Past "Celeste"

IT HAD BEEN TWO DAYS since my birthday. I had been talking to Eli as much as I could inconspicuously get away with. He was a lot different than what I had originally assumed he would be like. He was a sweetheart. I had stopped by my house so that I could quickly get changed and head to work. I couldn't wait to save a little more money.

I was beyond anxious to buy my first car. With the birthday money Eli had given me, it definitely enhanced my little savings account a lot. I probably could have purchased a little hoopty then, but I wanted something reliable. I didn't know how, but I had agreed to allow Eli to take me out on a date tonight. I was going to have to find a way to get Alicia to cover for me.

My mom had been a little on the depressed side lately and my father has been spending more time at the laundromats. All of which was fine by me because they weren't breathing down my neck as much. Thankfully, I hadn't been beaten or starved in a while. My mom had been staying in her room a lot and had been spending less time cooking and cleaning. Before leaving out the door I asked my mom if it were okay if I spent a night at Alicia's house, because we had an important project to work on. My mother quickly wiped her tear stained face and replied that she was okay with it.

She told me to call her after I got off and reached Alicia's house. Part of me wanted to comfort her and inquire about the tears. Although she had treated me as a sub-human for years, for some reason it still hurt me to see her hurting. I wished that I could somehow ease her pain and erase her sadness. However, I was already running late, and I did not want her to change her mind about me spending the night out. I quickly thanked her and rushed out of the door.

As I was walking down the driveway towards Alicia's car, I couldn't shake the feeling that I was being watched. I glanced to the right and noticed Shawn watching me from his window next door. I waved and smiled shyly as I thought about our encounter about a month ago.

∞

It was a Sunday and we had just gotten back home from church and having breakfast at Bob Evans. My dad had started drinking as soon as we entered the house and was becoming confrontational with my mother. That was my cue to get the hell out of dodge. I still had some studying to catch up on for a test we had scheduled for the next day at school. I gathered my textbooks and headed to my tree house. I had spent many days and some nights out here. I only wished that it came with a shower, fridge and a toilet. It was extremely spacious and peaceful.

After I had been studying for about an hour, I heard someone climbing up. I knew it could only be one person and that was Shawn. Alicia had never even been up here, because she was deathly afraid of heights. My parents never came up either. If anything, they would yell for me to come down. After a few moments, I noticed Shawn's curly hair pop into the entrance followed by his big dimpled smile.

Shawn was a cutie, but I never looked at him in a romantic way. I guess you could call him my best male friend.

Like Alicia, he knew about a lot of the things I encountered at home. He knew me extremely well and had comforted me more times than I care to remember over the years. He would also sneak me food a lot through my bedroom window when I was on food restrictions. My parents trusted him around me and he looked out for me like a big brother. He was now a college freshman, so I rarely got to hang out with him as much as I used to.

He usually came home every other weekend and on the major holidays. Our parents were pretty close, so naturally we had always clicked. Our parents took turns babysitting us growing up. His parents were strict as well, but not nearly as bad as mine were. Fortunately for him, his parents weren't abusive either. Shawn came up holding a frozen Caramello candy bar and a cream soda. He knew me so well. I jumped up and snatched the snacks from him and greedily ripped open the candy bar.

My stomach had immediately forgotten that I'd just eaten breakfast. People never understood how I could eat so much, yet never seem to gain any weight. What they didn't know was, there were plenty of days when I went without food. So, when I did have food, I overindulged. I guess some would call it binge eating. I loved Caramellos, especially frozen ones.

Shawn tilted his head to the side and replied, "Isn't this about a bitch?! Your little fat ass is going to come over here and snatch the food out of my hands and not even speak to a nigga? I see what you are on right now." He feigned tears as he walked closer.

I thought about my actions and fell out laughing. Normally I would've been embarrassed, but this was Shawn. I couldn't help it, whenever I saw my favorite candy bar, I behaved like a small child and had to have it. My parents rarely allowed me to eat candy. I stood up and walked over to my friend. I gave him the biggest hug and grabbed him by his ears. I then planted a bunch of friendly kisses all over his handsome face. I then apologized and thanked him for the snacks.

In an innocent, angelic voice I cooed, "Please forgive me? You know I love you!"

He replied, "Your hungry ass doesn't love me, you just want to get back to your candy. Go ahead."

I giggled and told him that I did want to get back to my candy, but that I still loved him. I went to give him another peck on the cheek when he turned his head and my lips landed on his. I gasped and blushed. Then I proceeded to apologize again. I sat down in front of my books and candy.

He asked, "Why do you keep apologizing Cee Cee? You know I'm just teasing you. I'm happy that my small gifts can bring you joy like that. That's why I love you, you appreciate the little things that I am able to do for you. I've missed your big-headed ass. There is nothing I wouldn't do for you. You know I got you. Plus, I turned my head on purpose."

I glanced at him and asked why.

Shawn and I had kissed before. With him being a couple of years older than me, he was always talking me into doing something crazy. In fact, we both shared our first kisses together. We had taught each other how to French kiss. That had been a while ago though and I never felt any sparks. I had even allowed Shawn to look at and fondle my small chocolate tits when we were younger. Our nasty asses even use to dry hump as kids. None of those things had ever done anything for me, but I suppose it helped his super curious ass out.

I remember one day after a sex education class I had asked Shawn if I could watch him jack off. I wanted to watch as his sperm erupted from his dick. I didn't think that he would agree, but to my surprise he had said yes. It was gross to watch, yet I couldn't look away. That's just how the two of us were. Neither of us were allowed to date so we only had each other to explore our curiosities with.

Shawn said, "I don't know why I did. I just felt like kissing your soft lips. It has been a while."

"Shawn, we are not kids anymore and we shouldn't be doing things like that anymore. We have adult bodies now and our actions can lead to adult consequences," I responded.

"Cee Cee, I want to ask you a couple of huge favors, but I don't want you to get mad at me, okay? Promise me," he coaxed.

"Shawn, you know I would do anything for you as well. Just ask me." I countered.

"Well, after the football game last week, me and some of the guys went out to celebrate. We all got on the subject of women, sex and stuff like that. They started teasing me because they know how my parents are and how they don't want me dating or having premarital sex. I'm a grown ass man and I feel as though I have to sneak around to pacify them. Sure, I could sneak around and date and to be honest, I have. The thing is, none of them are you. We've experienced all of our first sexual encounters together.

I know you may not be ready to go all the way, but when you are ready, I'd like for our first time to be together. I promise to wait for you, as long as you seriously take what I'm asking into consideration. I'd love for you to be my woman one day. Hell, my parents already love you with their picky asses!" He chuckled before continuing.

SHEENA PERRY

"But I don't want to pressure you into being with me right now knowing my school schedule will limit our time together. When...yes when, we decide to make us official, I want to have my shit together. I want to get you away from your punk ass parents. I don't have shit to offer you right now, but one day I hope to give you the world Cee Cee.

Anyway, that was my first question. The fellas said that I was strong as an ox because I don't get any pussy. They said that I was afraid of pussy and that I had never even smelled pussy before. At first, I was mad as hell until I realized that they were absolutely right. Not right about me being afraid of pussy. I am not afraid of pussy, but I have honestly never smelled pussy before. I would like to think that it does not smell like fish, onions or anything like a lot of the guys claim. If it does, why would they want it the way that they do?" He pondered out loud.

"So...so, my question is...and trust me I will completely understand if you aren't comfortable with..."

"Shawn get to the damn point already! What are you trying to ask me?" I impatiently questioned.

"Damn Cee Cee, why are you always interrupting me? I want to know if...if I can smell your pussy? There I asked!" He stated bashfully.

"Shawn, I think..."

"Man, see I knew you would say no! I let you watch me stroke my dick a while ago. No questions asked. You and your double standards! Celeste on the real, don't ask to see me do shit else!" He whined like an overgrown child.

I knew he was hot because he never called me Celeste.

"Shawn, shut the fuck up! You talk too damn much. I never said no. Calm down. You are turning red and your veins are popping out and shit. Your crybaby ass is about to morph into the Incredible Hulk and shit up in here. I was going to say, I think that your request is extremely strange, but if you would like to smell Ms. Kitty, then I will let you," I shrugged.

"I need a little time to answer your other question though. You've sprung a lot on me today," I continued.

A huge smile spread across his face and all I saw were white teeth and dimples. He truly was a good-looking guy. How had I never noticed before?

"Cee Cee, please tell me you did not name your cooch...?

"You don't have a pet name for your dick?" I interrupted with a naughty smirk.

"I do and maybe if you're lucky you'll find out what it is one day," he boasted.

I sucked my teeth and rolled my eyes hard as hell at his cocky ass.

"Whatever chump. So how do you want to do this weirdo? Do you want me to rub my pussy and then smell my fingers or do you actually want to sniff her?"

"Why do you have to say sniff man? You are really making me feel and sound like a perv. I want you to take off your panties. Lift up your dress and lay down. I want to look at it too. I've never seen a pussy before in person," he admitted.

"See you didn't say all of that shit now. I don't want you looking at my pussy like that. It's embarrassing! They are so ugly!"

"Come on Cee Cee, please. It's me, you know you can trust me. I would never judge you, laugh at you or tell anyone. I just really want to know what it smells and looks like," he pleaded literally on his knees.

"Fine, with your crybaby ass," I relented.

"Pull down your pants too. I don't want to be the only naked ass around here," I commanded.

He pulled me into a tight hug and kissed me passionately on my lips. For some odd reason, I didn't push him away. It felt amazing to be in his embrace. The only time that I ever came into physical contact with others is when I was being beaten into a bloody pulp.

He removed his sneakers. He then quickly unfastened his pants and in one swift motion pulled his pants and boxers down. He even pulled off his shirt and replied, "Is this naked enough?" I blushed and nodded.

I tried to look away, but his nude body had me in a trance. Shawn's body was perfect, and his dick was a lot bigger than I remembered. That muthafucka was in extremely close proximity to his knees. I proceeded to pull my dress up over my head. I rarely wore bras when I was at home...today was no different. I then slowly slid my panties down over my curvaceous hips. They were not Victoria Secrets, but thankfully they weren't the granny joints either.

I self-consciously tried to cover myself up as I noticed Shawn licking his thick pink lips and sizing me up from head to toe. He stepped forward and swept my long hair out of my face. He stared at me for what seemed like an eternity. He stated that I was so perfect. He leaned down as he lifted my chin and begin to kiss me. As he started to suck on my bottom lip and tongue, I felt his hard body press up against my unclad body. My hard nipples were beyond sensitive as they made contact with his warm flesh.

I broke our kiss and proceeded to lay down on the giant pink bean bag that I had in my tree house. He kneeled down in front of my legs that were clamped shut. He laughed and asked me to open my legs.

"How am I supposed to see and smell Ms. Kitty with your legs glued shut like that? Relax, I told you I got you."

I was shaking like a leaf and I had no idea why. Shawn climbed on top of me and started sucking and licking on my neck. I let out some involuntary moans, surprising even myself. I didn't even care if he left passion marks on my neck at that moment. He moved down and popped one of my Hershey kisses into his mouth. I gasped as he twirled his tongue skillfully around my nipples. He showed my girls equal attention as he swiftly darted back and forth.

My clit was throbbing, and my pussy was definitely making it rain. I was writhing from side to side unsure of how to react to all of these different sensations. I felt his hard-throbbing dick resting on my thighs and I shuddered. Shawn slowly snaked his tongue down to my belly button. I had my eyes clamped shut as I softly moaned his name.

I hadn't even realized that my legs were now spread wide apart until he replied, "Fuck I love the way your pussy smells. It definitely doesn't smell like fish or onions."

I suddenly grew self-conscious again with his pussy analysis. I pushed his head away and tried to close my legs again, but he didn't budge.

"Well, what does it smell like then?" I shyly asked.

"Honestly, I cannot compare the smell to anything else, but trust me it is a good clean smell. The smell is sexy as fuck and is turning me on like a muthafucka. I also love the way it looks. Cee Cee, you have a very pretty pussy. It is fat as fuck too from eating all of those Caramellos," he teased.

I was on the verge of mushing him in the forehead when I felt him suck my clit into his mouth. I screamed out in pleasure. I had never felt anything like that in my life! He watched for my reaction with his honey colored eyes. His eyes twinkled once he got the reaction he had hoped for. I arched my back as I lay there having pseudo-seizures.

I breathlessly asked Shawn what he was doing and reminded him that a taste test was not part of our deal. He responded by flicking his tongue up and down and from side to side. I was moaning so loudly that I am surprised that both sets of our parents hadn't come out to investigate my cries of pleasure.

On cue, Shawn hushed me. "Cee Cee hush, you are going to summon the entire neighborhood back here. Grab the back of my head if you need to or scream into the pillow. I grabbed the closest pillow and covered my mouth with it.

"Oh, shit Shawn, oohhhhh! Sssssss...that feels soooo fucking amazing. Oh God, please help me! This negro is trying to kill me," I whimpered into my pillow.

I grabbed Shawn's left index finger just as he was about to slide it inside of my juicy center. I had never even been penetrated by so much as a tampon, let alone a long ass finger. I was not ready for that. I almost lost it when Shawn plunged his tongue into my sweet pussy hole instead. The sounds of his slurping were intoxicating. In the midst of all of my moaning and Shawn's sloppy slurping, I had an overwhelming urge to pee.

I yelled, "Oh my God Shawn! Stop because I have to pee really really badly! I'm so..." Before I could finish my statement, Shawn jumped up in a panic.

If I wasn't so embarrassed it might have been funny. His monstrous dick was wildly bobbing up and down. His eyes were bulging out of his head while his lips and chin were lubricated with my pussy juices. Thankfully, as soon as he stopped, the urgency to urinate vanished. I slowly begin to redress.

Shawn sarcastically replied, "Heifer, did you seriously almost just pee in my mouth? Cee Cee, you are so nasty. That's the thanks I get for licking your little twat, hunh?"

I sat down and shrugged my shoulders as I finished off the rest of my Caramello and cream soda.

« Chapter 9 Special Friend »

The Past "Celeste"

I WONDERED WHY SHAWN was staring at me from his window like that. Maybe he was wanting to fulfill the other question that he had presented to me. If that was the case, then why didn't he just ask instead of lurk around. I had been so busy lately with the new job that I hadn't seen a lot of him since the tree house incident. I missed him and prayed that there wouldn't be any weirdness between us. I was happy that the urge to urinate interrupted us when it did. The good Lord only knows how far things would've gone had we not been forced to stop.

I jumped into Alicia's moms' car and she quickly sped off in the direction of the mall. She was excited that my mother had agreed to me spending the night at her house. I had initially suggested a double date because I knew that I was going to be nervous being around Eli alone. She however felt that Eli and I needed some alone time since this was our official first date. She made an excellent point, but I was still nervous.

After arriving at the mall, she agreed to pick me up after work. I thanked her and told her I'd see her later tonight. After clocking in, I said my hellos to everyone. I really did love my job. I know a lot of people who dreaded going to work and only worked for the paycheck. I can honestly say that I would have worked at Divas R Us for free. Most of the customers were great.

My coworkers were slowly but surely becoming my friends and my boss, Joe, had been a true Godsend.

I was starting to feel as if my job was a home away from home. Hell, I spent more time with my coworkers than I did with my own miserable family. We were pretty busy which was to be expected for a Friday evening. I knew that the busier we were, meant the faster time would seem to go by. Before I knew it, I would be on my first official date. Thinking about Eli and our date gave me butterflies. I was smiling and fantasizing about my date with Eli as I arranged our new items on the racks. I also thought about Shawn and what our last encounter meant. I could not deny my newfound attraction to him.

Had I not stumbled across Eli, I would have probably agreed to make Shawn my first already. He seemed like an obvious first choice. Now that I was dating Eli, things were now so complicated. I felt more comfortable with Shawn because we were practically raised together, but I also knew that he wasn't ready to be with me either. He was away at school and I'm sure he was around lots of beautiful college girls.

I felt somewhat guilty and conflicted. Shawn was safe and familiar, while Eli was new and mysterious. I was no fool, I was pretty sure that Eli was still seeing other girls besides me. I knew it wasn't my place to get upset, but I felt some type of way about it. We had never discussed dating each other exclusively, so I guess we were both free to explore other options.

Deep in my thoughts, I barely noticed Joe as he walked up behind me. He proceeded to ask me to step into his office. I threw a questioning look at my coworker Ashleigh, but she simply shrugged her shoulders. I had never had a job before, and I prayed that I wasn't in trouble for anything. I felt that I had been doing a great job around there.

Once entering Joe's small office, he asked that I close the door behind me. I obliged.

He observed me with a serious expression on his face for a few moments as I begin to stammer, "Joe, I hope that I am not being fi...fir...fired. I have been trying my hardest around here. I love my job and wh...what...whatever I did wrong please let me fix..."

He held his hand up instantly silencing me.

"Celeste, that is not why I brought you in here. You are not fired. In fact, I wanted to commend you on the excellent work that you are doing around here. You have not been here long, but I can already tell that you are cut from a different cloth, so to speak. You are not just here for a paycheck and that shows in the quality of your work. You have certainly impressed me. If you keep up the good work, I am confident that you will make assistant manager in no time."

I gasped, but remained silent so Joe continued.

"To show my appreciation, I am bumping your pay up to eight dollars an hour. Also, I noticed that it was your birthday a couple of days ago. You've been off, so I haven't been able to give you your present."

I was speechless and ecstatic to say the very least. This was truly the last thing that I had expected to hear today. Joe stood up and walked over to me. He stood behind me and began to massage my shoulders. My body instantly tensed up. I decided to play it cool and see where this was going.

He then started talking again. "I knew when you first came in here to apply for the job that you were special. You carry yourself respectfully and with class. You are beyond gorgeous, but I suspect that all your little boyfriends tell you that all the time. I want you to know that I am always here for you should you ever need anything. Consider me your special friend...not just your boss, okay?"

I simply nodded my head yes.

He stopped massaging my shoulders and handed me an elongated black box. I took the black box and opened it. I gasped and covered my mouth with my right hand when I noticed an incredibly beautiful, expensive diamond encrusted necklace with matching earrings. My name and birthday were engraved into the necklace along with the words *"With love, your special friend"*.

I glanced up at him with wide eyes and shook my head. I handed the box back to Joe and told him that I could not accept such an expensive gift. I told him it was not necessary and that a little card would have sufficed.

"Nonsense, you are worth every penny that this cost and so much more. In time, you will get more. There is plenty where this came from. Let me put this on you. Once I saw this set, I knew it would look beautiful on you." Joe announced.

I surrendered and allowed Joe to put the jewelry on me. I was not raised to disobey my elders. I didn't want to continue to seem ungrateful. I turned to Joe and gave him a hug as I thanked him. Joe pulled me and held me tightly. He whispered that it was a pleasure with his lips resting up against my neck.

He softly kissed my neck as I pulled away from him. I had felt his penis poking up against my abdomen. Now that we were no longer hugging, a little tenting was noticeable in his black slacks. I couldn't help but to be disgusted. I asked Joe if there was anything else, because I had a lot of inventory to stock. He told me that we were finished so I briskly returned to work.

After my meeting with Joe I couldn't help but have conflicting feelings. I was excited that he thought so highly of me and viewed me as potential management material. I believed that I was an exceptionally hard worker and it felt amazing to receive recognition for it. I was happy with the company and felt that the pay was great. He often encouraged me to do well in school and was a saint for working around my school schedule. For some reason our encounter left me a little unsettled.

I definitely felt as if he were making a pass at me. I knew that he was married not only because of his wedding ring, but also because of the photographs of his family in his office. In the pictures, they both looked so happy. He had two small sons as well. They both looked a lot like him. I knew he found me attractive based off of the hard on he had during and after our hug. Prior to our meeting, I had never had any indications that he was attracted to me in that way.

Sure, he spent a lot of time with me over the past month, but he was the one who had personally trained me. I was aware that his attraction to me was inappropriate as well as illegal. However, I knew it wouldn't go anywhere so I wouldn't snitch on him. I didn't want him getting into any trouble on my account. I would just avoid being alone with him at all costs. How did I go from no love interests to three over the span of a month? One thing was for sure, his old ass dick would never ever be introduced to Ms. Kitty.

« Chapter 10 The First Date »

The Past "Celeste"

ELI LOOKED SO SEXY tonight. He was dressed casually, yet his presence commanded attention. I could tell that he had recently received a fresh line up. His goatee was also trimmed to perfection. His eyes were low and glazed over as usual, so I knew that he had recently inhaled some cannabis. I had opted to wear some white high waisted jeans with a pink crop top that snugly showcased my boobs. My feet were clad in pink peep toe heels and my clutch matched my shirt and heels to perfection.

My newly acquired jewelry from Joe adorned my neck and ears. It was beginning to get a little cold out, so I threw a cute little cardigan over my shoulders. Eli was full of surprises. He actually came and knocked on Alicia's door unlike a lot of the boys from our generation. From our many conversations, he had learned many of my likes and dislikes. He knew that I loved pink and white. So of course, he showed up with two dozen pink roses and two dozen white roses. Instead of those disgusting 'guess what's inside of me' chocolates, he bought me seventeen Caramellos to represent the number of years I had been on this Earth.

He had a couple of pairs of expensive heels whose brand I am sure I couldn't pronounce, two bags filled with items from Victoria's Secret items and a pink pager. I was so impressed and so excited about all my late birthday gifts. I had wondered why he had asked me my shoe size the other day. I had told him several times that he didn't have to get me anything...but I am happy as hell that he did not listen to my ass. I couldn't believe that I had a pager!

I must have thanked Eli over a hundred times before he told me he had been thanked enough for a lifetime. I put all my gifts in Alicia's room and told her that I was heading out. She was a little bummed because Mike had broken their date tonight. He told her that his parents had grounded him because his grades were slipping in two classes. He was on the verge of being kicked off the various sports teams that he participated in because of this. That was a no-no because he was hoping to be offered a football or basketball scholarship for college.

My girl looked so pitiful that I had asked her if she wanted me to cancel my plans and make it a girl's night. She looked at me as if I had lost my mind.

"Cee Cee, do you not see all these fabulous gifts in this room? If you do not go out with Eli's fine ass right now, I am going to, bitch!" I laughed at her silliness and told her I wouldn't be gone too long.

She waved me off. After walking out of the house, I was reunited with Eli who opened the car door for me. He complimented me on how good I looked and smelled. I blushed because I still couldn't believe that someone like him would be interested in someone like me. He could have any woman that he wanted, yet he wanted to be with me. His ride was nice! He had a fully loaded 1994 cocaine white Cadillac. I was in love with his car. The interior was peanut butter colored and smelled brand spanking new. He had his name etched on the headrests.

We had both decided against seeing a movie. It was a terrible place to carry out a first date. You could not talk freely and get to know one another. To dinner we went. I told him that I had been dying to hit up this spot on Delmar Blvd called The

Melting Pot. I had always heard that it was pretty good and specialized in fondue. It was however a little on the expensive side. He stated that he loved the restaurant and looked forward to going again. We arrived and was met by a nice little crowd, but we didn't have to wait long before we were seated.

Eli and I were thoroughly enjoying ourselves while people watching. He was hilarious as he talked about the workers and other patrons mercilessly. The food was amazing, and I couldn't remember the last time I had laughed this much.

I asked Eli, "You seem like such a great guy, why on Earth are you single? What is wrong with you? Do your feet stink or something?" I was very serious, but he doubled over in a fit of laughter.

"Naw baby, every part of me smells spic and span. I just haven't found any of the women that I've come across to be wifey material. A lot of these women expect me to give them the utmost respect and place them on this pedestal when they don't even love and respect themselves. If I was just a regular old nigga most of their asses wouldn't even pay my yella ass no mind. They see the money, the cars, the good hair and they drop their little funky panties. If they cannot get to me then one of my partners will smash.

I'm tired of that same old shit. That's why I am here with you. You are very different. You march to your own beat. Not only are you drop-dead gorgeous, but you are smart as hell. I see yo ass collecting them damn nerd awards at school. Celeste, *you* are wifey material. I'm really feeling yo little ass, shorty. I want you to be my girl from now on. That pussy belongs to me. You have never given *my* pussy away, have you? I want to be the only one to ever feel you on that level."

As I was about to respond to Eli's admission, I noticed a couple of familiar faces a few booths away. I simply could not believe the audacity of this asshole. He was sitting in the booth with some ratchet ass heifer who wasn't even cute. I shook my head at this fool who seemed to be having a good old time. His stupid ass sat there laughing it up and shit while my best friend spent this Friday night sad and alone at home. Furthermore, if you must cheat at least 'cheat up'.

This bitch didn't hold a candle to my best friend. She was high yellow with the worst skin I had ever seen. She had a big gap in between her yellow ass two front teeth. She adorned the heaviest and fakest looking eye lashes ever. I don't know how she was able to keep her eyes open with those dingy fuckers resting halfway down her cheeks.

Whoever did the poor child's weave needed their asses slapped! The bitch looked like a cross between a nappy peacock and an orangutan. Maybe her head and pussy game were good. She was loud as fuck and beyond hood. I almost lost it when she leaned down and kissed him on the lips before excusing herself. Mike seemed pissed off about the kiss too. As she stood up, I had to admit, home girl did have a nice ass shape. But so did Alicia.

By this time, Eli had also noticed what I was focusing on. I had pulled out my voice recorder that I often used during my lectures and I waited for the wildebeest to return. I was about to become inspector Gadget in this bitch and collect all the evidence I needed to hang him by his unfaithful balls. When she returned to their booth, she stood in front of him and wrapped her scrawny arms around the back of his head. All while he reached around and squeezed her jiggly, loose ass booty. I heard her giggle once he loudly smacked her ass.

I was crossly burning a hole through them both. I hadn't even noticed that Shrek had observed me glaring at them. Her eyes were wild as she nervously tapped him on the shoulder. The ugly bitch must have recognized that I was his girlfriend's best friend. He slowly turned around and I smirked as his eyes too doubled in size. The nigga looked like he had just hit an eight ball.

He jumped up and quickly made his way over to the booth that Eli and I shared. I discreetly pressed record on my voice recorder. Eli put his hand on mine and asked me to keep it cool. I nodded. I was a class act, so I was not about to allow either one of those fuckers to bring me out of character.

As Mike nervously stood next to our booth with the camel looking hoe by his side, Eli was the first to speak. "Sup bro, are you lost? Can we help you with something?"

Mike responded, "Eli man, I was just wanting to know if I could holla at Cee Cee for a minute outside?"

I waved him off dismissively.

"Mike, I am not interested in hearing shit that you have to say in here or out there," I replied pointing towards the door.

I continued, "Maybe I need glasses or something because she sure does not look anything like Alicia. Seriously Mike, look at home girl over there and look at Alicia. I don't even think the two of them come from the same species. How am I in good faith supposed to share this mess with my friend? The biggest insult in all of this isn't even the fact that your lying cheating ass is out here creeping on Alicia, but the fact that you didn't have the common decency to at least creep with someone halfway in my girl's lane. I am so disappointed in your black ass. Just get away from this table. Don't you see we are on a date?!"

My teeth were clenched, and my voice was laced with venom. The nerve of these two! Ms. Ratchet's scary ass didn't say shit to me even after I had taken numerous shots at her unattractive appearance. I was beginning to like her ugly ass less and less by the second.

"Come on sis, don't be like that. It isn't what it looks like for real yo. I called Sha'Keisha out here so that she could help me study. You know how I feel about Alicia. You already know don't none of these bitches even compare to my baby. Do me a favor and please do not tell her about you seeing us here. I do not want to cause her any unnecessary stress. I only have eyes for her." Mike pleaded.

Sha'Keisha looked genuinely hurt by Mike's revelation, but she remained quiet as she lowered her colorful head. "You were studying, hunh? Well, where the hell are your books Mike?!" I quizzed skeptically.

"I made it halfway here when I realized that I had left them on my kitchen table. Since I was almost here and had made reservations, I just kept it pushing," he lied.

The shit sounded so dumb and convenient that even Eli busted out laughing while shaking his head.

I responded with finality, "Mike I am giving you tonight to break this to my sister and then leave her the fuck alone. I have all the evidence that I need. I have been recording this entire wack ass exchange between us. She deserves so much better than your trifling ass. I truly do hope that you man up and tell her about this bullshit, so that I don't have to. This is your mess and I'd appreciate it if you cleaned it up. Again, I am on a date so step the fuck away from our booth!"

Mike looked as if he wanted to say something else, but had change his mind after the look Eli shot his way. He looked like a sad ass puppy that had lost his best friend as he turned and walked away. He threw some crumpled bills on the table. They hadn't even had the opportunity to eat their expensive meal. He turned and glanced at me once more with a pleading look in his eyes before exiting through the door.

I was pissed off because Mike and his bullshit antics had ruined what had started out as the perfect date. I really hoped that Mike told Alicia about his whorish ways so that I didn't have to. I really didn't want to be the one to tell her about Mike cheating, but as her best friend I would if I had to. I was serious when I told him that he only had until the morning. Eli asked if I were okay and if I wanted to leave. I told him that I was okay and wanted to continue with our date.

I then stated, "In response to your question...you know, about me being yours? Can I have a little time to think about it? I just want to be cautious and protect myself from bullshit like that. Please don't be mad. I want you to understand where I'm coming from."

For a split moment, he appeared upset, however the expression disappeared so quickly that I thought I had imagined it.

He looked me in my eyes and sincerely replied, "Of course, beautiful. I will give you all the time you need, just don't make me wait too long. I'd never do any fuck boy shit like that to you. Our chemistry is out of this world and I just want you to be my queen. I would never hurt you."

I nodded and promised I would give him an answer tomorrow after my emotions were under control. We finished our meal and headed for the door.

He seductively replied, "I still have one more present for you, but due to such short notice I need more time to get it together for you. You're going to love this shit too, bae."

I laughed and mushed him as I told him he was a trip. He was so amazing and always full of surprises. He was attentive and considerate of my wants and needs. I couldn't wait to find out what my next surprise would be. I really liked Eli and I just prayed that he didn't turn out to be anything like Mike's community dick having ass.

« Chapter 11 Welcome Home »

Present Day "Autumn"

TODAY I WAS FINALLY being discharged from the loony hospital. I was so excited about leaving those crazy ass kids behind. After receiving the few personal items that I had been admitted with, I was escorted out of the heavy locked doors. I had met a woman named Kelly who had introduced herself as my case worker. She wore a cheap two-piece suit and a tired wig. Kelly appeared as if she would rather be anywhere, but with my ass at that very moment.

She was pleasant enough towards me, but I could tell that all the smiles she flashed in my direction were forced. She told me that I was going to be placed in the Douglas household. Kelly explained that Mrs. Douglas was a widowed older woman who had one adult biological child. He remained in the house to assist her with the foster children. She had been fostering children for over twenty-five years and was well respected within the community.

She and her late husband had planned on having a large family; however, after having her son she was unable to conceive again. Thus, she and her husband decided to open their home to children in need. She sounded like a saint. I breathed a huge sigh of relief as we pulled up to a beautiful house surrounded by a well-manicured lawn. The house was no mansion, but I'm sure Mrs. Douglas had spent a small fortune to reside in this quiet little community in Chesterfield.

Maybe living out here wouldn't be so bad. Perhaps I could even convince Mrs. Douglas to foster Wintress as well so that we could be reunified. I missed her so damn much. I just had to find her and at least talk to her and see if she was okay. Upon exiting the cramped car, I noticed than an older white woman had stepped onto the porch followed by a short pudgy white guy. They both wore huge welcoming smiles on their faces and waved for us to come on up. I could smell something delicious baking once reaching the porch.

The older woman introduced herself as Mrs. Douglas and she announced that the fat guy was her son, Donald. He quickly reintroduced himself as *'Don'* and grabbed the little Schnucks grocery bag that contained my pathetic little life. He appeared to be about my late mother's age, which was mid-30's. I guessed Mrs. Douglas to be around her late-50's to early-60's.

I flashed them both a shy smile and stated, "My name is Autumn and I am pleased to meet you both. Thank you so much for welcoming me into your home. I will not be a problem, I promise."

Mrs. Douglas flashed a genuine smile and stated, "I am pleased to meet you too Autumn. You are pretty enough to be a model; do you know that? I was thrilled when I received a call about possibly having a girl placed. For the past three years, I have only received little boys. Boys are fine, but sometimes, it is nice to have another woman around the house. Let me warn you, we are outnumbered," she gushed.

I giggled as we all stepped into her beautifully decorated home.

I looked around in amazement. I had never been inside of any home that was remotely as beautiful as this one. All I've known were the cramped little apartments that I had become accustomed to. I couldn't believe that I had lucked up and would be living here with these nice people. Mrs. Douglas asked if either Kelly or I were hungry. Before I could lie and tell her that I wasn't, my stomach growled loudly revealing the truth for me.

Everyone lightly chuckled as Mrs. Douglas stated, "I will take that as a yes."

The truth was, the hospital food was not that great. However, even if it were, I've been so down lately that I haven't had an appetite. Mrs. Douglas and Don had made heaping plates for the four of us. She was a remarkable cook. She explained that there were two other little boys that lived in the house, but currently they were both at school. She promised I would meet them later that day. We sat and ate for a while. Then we became more acquainted with one another.

Mrs. Douglas had revealed that her late husband Donald Sr had died eight years prior from lung cancer. His cancer had slowly metastasized to various organs before also taking over his bones. She still seemed to be mourning her loss. My heart went out to Mrs. Douglas because I knew firsthand how badly losing someone close hurt. She did express how compassionate and attentive the hospice nurses were to them during his transition.

She laid out the house rules and told me what her expectations of me were. They were all reasonable. I gave her an abbreviated version of why I was now an occupant in her home. I hinted around at possibly being reunited with Wintress. I also inquired about whether my mother would be having a funeral. Both Kelly and Mrs. Douglas promised me that they would look into both matters for me.

My room was huge! I glanced around in awe at its massive size. My bed had to be at least queen-sized and I wasn't even sharing it. Wintress and I had always shared a full-sized bed. I had my own 32-inch tv and my room came with all the necessities as well as non-essentials that a teenage girl could wish for. I walked over to my newly acquired closet and noticed that it was already filled with various styles of clothing in my size. I noticed the rows of shoes neatly lined up against the walls as well.

"Whoever picked out these items has great taste," I thought out loud.

I almost shit on myself when a masculine voice whispered behind me, "I'm glad you like everything. I picked out most of these clothes. I figured it was what teenage girls are into these days. Kelly told us your sizes and we quickly got to work in here."

"Thank you so much for everything. It is perfect Don!" I shrieked.

"Oh, before I head out, here is your phone. The kids are crazy about these phones today. Your new number is on this post-it note. I have already programmed my number as well as my mother's number into the phone. I hope you like it. Welcome home Celeste!" He smiled and retreated from my room.

My eyes bucked once I noticed that he had handed me a new IPhone 7 plus! He was certainly strange, but I could live with a *little* strange. Couldn't I?

I laid on top of my plush bed recounting the day's events until sleep took over me. I must have felt the presence of someone standing over me because my eyes flew open and I stumbled out of my bed...falling flat on my ass. I then noticed two of the most handsome little boys ever. They were looking at me curiously as I pulled myself up off the floor.

I spoke first. "Hi, my name is Autumn, and it's nice to meet you two. I'm going to be living here for a while and I hope we can become great friends. What are your names?"

The little chocolate boy with the long curly lashes spoke first.

"My name is Chris and I'm seven years old. This is my big brother Landon," he stated pointing at the blonde-haired, blue-eyed boy standing next to him.

"Well, we are not real-life brothers because I am black and he is white, but I love him just like a real brother," he innocently elaborated.

"How old are you Landon?" I asked turning my attention to the other boy.

Landon did not speak, however, he held up nine little fingers.

"Landon cannot hear or talk. I overheard Momma Douglas telling his new caseworker that his real momma did a lot of drugs and made him like this. He can read lips really good though and he knows sign language. Do you know any sign language Autumn?" Chris inquired.

"Unfortunately, I don't, but I would love to learn some. I will see if I can take some classes so that I can learn," I promised.

After conversing with the two boys for a while, Mrs. Douglas had summoned us to come down for supper. I could certainly get use to this. When I lived with my mom, I was responsible for the cooking, cleaning and any other miscellaneous chores. The Douglas family had hired help to assist with such tasks. However, she insisted on doing all the cooking.

She enjoyed cooking. I had learned that Douglas Sr had come from old money. They had the house built from scratch prior to him receiving his inheritance. They had fallen in love with this house so much so that even after receiving a large portion of money, they refused to move into a larger home that better represented their enormous bank accounts. They had made several upgrades to their home over the years; however, Mrs. Douglas only had eyes for her current home.

She stated that this house had their personal touches and embodied who they truly were. I admired her a lot. She wasn't stuck up and bourgeois as I'm sure many people assumed, she was. She was personable and was like the grandmother I never had. She was an attractive older woman and I knew that she was probably gorgeous in her prime. My suspicions were verified after visualizing dozens of photos and portraits of Mrs. Douglas in varying stages of her life. Her late husband was quite the catch too.

I noticed lots of photos around of Don along with other children they had fostered over the years. I couldn't help but to shudder. How could two extremely tall and attractive people create such a short, dumpy and unattractive offspring? The funny thing is he strongly resembled them both, but he had his own fugly twist...yes F.U.G.L.Y twist. He was fucking ugly!

Later that day, Mrs. Douglas informed me that my mother's funeral was scheduled to be held in two days. She stated that someone had anonymously paid for the entire service in full. Deep down I presumed that she was the anonymous person. I could not think of anyone else who would have foot the bill. We didn't have any family and my mother had created more enemies than allies in her final years.

Mrs. Douglas then divulged that my little sister would be

present. I gleefully pranced around the living room with so much excitement that you would have thought I had been discussing winning the lottery, instead of my mother's funeral arrangements. Although it hadn't been quite a week since my mother's ill-fated demise, I felt as if I hadn't seen Wintress in years. Despite our obvious age gap, she was truly my best friend.

She depended on me...she needed me. I now realized that I needed her just as much. I just prayed that the family that she was with was half as nice as the family I was placed with. I couldn't wait for Mrs. Douglas to finally bring her home with us. I knew that she'd love her just as I did. Tomorrow Mrs. Douglas was going to enroll me into a high school in her district. I loved school and hated that I had fallen behind this week while I was in the hospital. She told me that she was going to allow me to miss school tomorrow and I would just start fresh on Monday. I was okay with that.

∞

Saturday rolled around and I was preparing myself for my mother's funeral. I was mourning and hurting of course due to her death, but more so because of the domino effect of events that had followed. I just wished that this was all one big prank or a bad dream. I knew that I would never be so lucky. I still found it hard to believe that I would never see my mother again after today. I would never again hear her sweet voice or infectious laughter. She was gone forever...forever was an extremely long time.

She was not perfect, but she did the best she could considering her spirit had been broken. Men had broken her down many times throughout her life. One gave her a death sentence while another one eventually took her life. What gave these assholes the right?! Don jarred me from my thoughts as he informed me that the limo was outside waiting for us.

I had asked that everyone wear white. I didn't want to be surrounded by dark depressing ass clothing. Everyone was great about it. I had obtained the number to the house where Wintress was living yesterday. When I first heard her little voice, my heart skipped a beat. She sounded so happy when she answered the phone. She immediately became tearful once she'd discovered that it was me on the other end.

As she cried, she expressed that she had thought the EMTs and cops had killed me by the way that I was tackled and landed on the ground. I choked down my own tears and assured her that I was very much alive and well. I told her about our mother's arrangements on Saturday and ask her to see if her foster family could get her a white dress for her services.

I told her about the family that I was staying with and let her know that I was doing everything in my power to get her moved to where I was. She reported that the family that she was with treated her well, but she missed me. She stated that home was where I was and that made me feel saddened yet loved at the same time. I gave her my cellphone number and I told her to call me anytime...day or night if she needed me for anything. We said our goodbyes and I love 'yous' prior to disconnecting the call.

The next day we walked into the nearly empty church. I noticed a few faces that I recognized, but not many. Some of them were fellow drug addicts coming to pay their respect. Most of the people present did not know my mother personally. They had heard about her death via the news and came to express their condolences. I scanned the crowd for one face in particular and smiled once I found who I was looking for.

I ran in my white five-inch heels to my baby sis. She looked so beautiful and I could've sworn she had grown a couple of inches in my absence. I was the mirror image of my mother at her age. I had a beautiful mocha color with dimples for days. I had long lashes and naturally arched eyebrows. My jet-black hair cascaded down my smooth back. I was short just as my mother had been with the perfect hourglass figure.

The only thing that I seemed to have inherited from that deadbeat father of mine, was my light hazel eyes. It was striking to many that such beautiful light eyes were sported by someone of my skin tone. I was accused of wearing contacts a lot, but I knew the truth, so I never bothered to entertain those skeptical individuals.

My sister on the other hand did not resemble me and my mother much, aside from the long hair. I assumed that she must look like her father...whoever that muthafucka is. She was definitely mixed with something. She looked Hispanic, but I was not sure. She was a beautiful child and I knew that she would grow to be a stunning woman. She was tall as well. At eight she was nearly as tall as I was at fifteen going on sixteen.

She looked as if she had been crying. I wiped her face and told her to be strong because that would be what our mother wanted. She wouldn't want us crying over her death. In her words, "What do spilled tears solve?"

I introduced her to the Douglas clan and she immediately hit it off with Chris and Landon. I also had the opportunity to meet the Price family. They were a young African American couple who had been experiencing issues with fertility. They had recently decided to foster a child with the possibility of eventually adopting. Wintress was the first child that they had placed with them. They seemed crazy about my little sister, but they simply could not have her. She belonged with me at the Douglas house.

We made our way to my mother's casket and I must admit she looked extremely peaceful. In her final days, she had become emaciated and appeared to be in constant pain. Now lying supine in her final bed, she looked very beautiful. She looked identical to the picture that we had sitting next to her casket. In the picture, she was so youthful...and innocent. She had her entire life ahead of her.

The makeup they put on her was flawless and well blended. I hated going to funerals and seeing the deceased with excessive makeup on giving them an unnatural appearance. Observing my mother as she appeared to only be taking a nap gave me great comfort.

I whispered to my mother, "I haven't forgotten my promise to you mommy. I love you and I am so sorry that this happened to you."

I kissed her cold, stiff cheek as I willed myself not to cry in front of all those people. Once I felt that I had my emotions under control, I took a seat in the front row next to Wintress. I looked on as a few people came and shared their fond memories of my mother. Involuntary tears streamed down my face as my old next-door neighbor, Skye sang "Take Me to the King." I absolutely loved this song. Skye's voice was so rich and powerful. She most certainly gave Tamela Mann a run for her money. I truly appreciated her coming today.

After Skye finished singing, it was my turn to recite a poem that I'd written years ago during the mist of one of my mother's abusive relationships. I was so emotional that I wasn't sure that I'd be able to prevent my voice from wavering. As I slowly walked past my mother, I deliberately refrained from looking at her. I would have lost it had I looked at her. Peering at everyone from the podium, I took a moment to gather my thoughts.

To calm my nerves, I focused on my sister. I knew she'd get me through the most difficult time of my life.

Clearing my throat, I stated, "I truly appreciate you all for coming and showing your support today. My mom had a rough life, but she was always a good woman. She wasn't the perfect mother, but I do believe that she tried. She battled with severe depression and abused drugs to cope with her emotional and physical pain. She had so much to offer the world. As badly as I wish she were here with us, I know God has bigger plans for her. Apparently, he needs her more. I find solace in the fact that she is no longer suffering.

I watched my mother go from one bad relationship to the next. I never understood how someone who was so intelligent could make so many terrible decisions when it came to their personal life. I've witnessed her suffer insurmountable abuse at the hands of her boyfriends. A few years ago, I wrote a little poem that I feel is appropriate for this unfortunate gathering. Please bear with me as I dedicate this poem to my dear mother."

I looked around the church while inwardly praying that I would be able to get through the day. I just wanted that day to end. Clearing my parched throat, I begin to recite the poem from memory.

"Swollen Lips,

And Broken Hips,

Black and Blue Eyes,

And Beaten Thighs,

A Bloody Nose,

And Displaced Toes,

Missing Teeth,

And Battered Feet,

Worn-out Knees,

A Misused Spleen,

Pleasing Cries,

And Wish He Dies,

Unheard Screams,

All Too Familiar Dreams,

Unshed Tears,

And Persistent Fears,

A Lost Soul,

And Forgotten Goals,

Angels Pray,

As We Lay You Away,"

Wallowing in my grief, I was unaware of the fact that I had fallen to my knees and was crying inconsolably. I cried like a newborn baby. I hadn't cried in years and didn't think the tears would ever stop. My heart hurt so bad. I never knew pain like this existed. Why did God allow such misery and heartache to occur? I was having a difficult time understanding this. The reality of the permanence of death consumed me. My sister had walked on stage to embrace me.

We both sorrowfully cried and tuned out our concerned audience. They didn't understand our pain. They just couldn't relate. For the life of me, I couldn't understand why they pretended to. Once I was all cried out, I finally stood up. Attempting to compose myself, I accepted some Kleenex's from Mrs. Douglas. My eyes were so swollen that I could barely see.

Glancing around, my eyes met with an extremely handsome guy. He appeared to be around my mother's age, and I wondered if he personally knew her or if he had heard about her on the news. Somehow, he seemed familiar. I felt as if I knew him from somewhere.

Noticing my gaze, he smiled and mouthed the words, "I am praying for you and your sister. Keep your head up Autumn."

I nodded in acknowledgement at his kind words of encouragement. At that moment, I heard a baby sounding off loudly. Diverting my attention away from the handsome man, I noticed my sorry ass sperm donor. I guess he'd decided to come and pay his unwelcomed condolences. After spotting me, he swiftly made his way over to me with my alleged little sister, Justice.

She was a beautiful baby. She had inherited his eyes as well. As I looked back and forth between the two of them, I noticed that his new wife was noticeably absent. He pulled me in for a hug, but I didn't bother hugging his cowardly ass back.

"Autumn, please don't be like that. I love you and as your parent I made the decision that I felt was best for everyone. I just wanted to stop by to give my condolences for your mother. How are you Sweet Pea? Janet was unable to accompany us because she couldn't get the day off on such short notice. I also wanted you to meet your baby sister."

He proudly held Justice up and excitedly cooed, "Hey Justice, this is Autumn, your big sister! Yes, she is!"

I rolled my eyes and felt bad about rejecting an innocent baby, but fuck them both and his bitch of a wife.

"Micah, why are you and this half-bred baby at my mother's funeral? You don't give a shit about me and you made that abundantly clear during our last conversation. I came to you as your flesh and blood and asked you to do me one solid favor.

Hell, it isn't even a favor it is your parental duty! You chose your new bitch and your new baby over me. You have never done shit for me my entire life! As far as I am concerned, my only parent is laying over there in that pretty pink and white box. I only have one sister and she is standing over there," I spazzed, pointing at Wintress.

"You are dead to me! I don't need your pathetic condolences, so you can leave! Get out and take her crying ass with you!!!" I shrieked, startling Justice.

In that moment, I didn't give a shit. I was breathing heavily, and my nostrils were flared like an angry bull.

I heard his stupid ass mutter, "I am so sorry Autumn. My intentions weren't to upset you at all. I have always tried to do right by you. I gave your mom four hundred dollars a month to help take care of you. I did what I could for you. Do not discredit my efforts in parenting you!"

I was seeing red by this time and I no longer wanted to entertain any of these clowns in here. I crudely bumped into his ass, not giving two fucks about that baby he was holding. I hugged my one and *only* little sister tightly.

I promised to call her later in the evening before yelling, "Take me home! Get me the hell away from that asshole!" I swiftly switched my shapely toned ass up out of that church.

« Chapter 12 Pass the Wipes Please »

The Past "Eli"

"**MY NIGGAS, WHEN I** tell y'all that I was ready to fuck Mike's big ass up!!! I had Cee Cee hanging on every single word that I was slinging her way. His big goofy ass just had to come in that muthafucking restaurant fucking my shit up with that busted down hoe," I complained swiping my hands down my face in a vexed manner.

I have standards and haven't personally busted Sha'Keisha's pussy open, but I knew shorty's body count was probably higher than mine. I knew a bunch of niggas from around the way that had slid up into that loose shit. Apparently, my homies thought what I was saying was funny, because they were laughing so hard several of them had tears streaming down their faces.

"Well I am happy that I could amuse you sons of bitches! I'm over here pouring my heart out to you ugly ass niggas and y'all are laughing like I'm Richard Pryor up in this bitch!" I replied with a serious expression fixed on my face.

I still had plenty of time to seal my deal with little Ms. Cee Cee, but a nigga was getting restless. Don't get me wrong, I was getting pussy every day. I was buried balls deep in a pussy or two on a daily basis. However, I was ready to sample *her* pussy. It seemed like the more she turned me down, the more I craved what I'd never had before.

We were a week into the deal, and I had taken her out almost every night. I spoiled her rotten by getting her everything she so much as glanced at from her peripheral vision. It certainly wasn't even about winning the money anymore, because I had tricked that off and so much more on her little sexy ass.

I know I may seem bipolar as hell, but my feelings and ego were a little bruised when she didn't immediately jump at the chance to be my girl. I mean I didn't want a girlfriend or no shit like that, but when I ask a bitch to be my lady, I expected them to graciously accept my offer. She had me feeling some type of way about that, 'I'll think about it bullshit.' I was a sexy ass nigga...she better recognize that shit.

Last night I had taken her to a drive-in theater in Belleville, Illinois. We were kissing and I had her little thick ass straddling my lap. This is the most physical contact the she had ever allowed me to have with her and I damn sure wasn't going to stop her. I knew she wasn't going to let me hit it in my truck, especially with it being her first time. I honestly wouldn't respect her if she did. Again, I know I'm bipolar as fuck. I did, however, want to see how far she was willing to go.

I went to lift her shirt up so that I could gain access to her mouthwatering titties. She quickly darted her paranoid ass eyes around and told me 'no' because we were in a public parking lot with dozens of other people around. I reminded her that I had tinted windows and that no one could see us. She appeared to relax and proceeded to release her death grip from around my wrists. I smirked because it was cute that she thought her little grip could stop me.

I went back to lifting up her shirt and as I went to unclasp her bra with one hand she flinched in pain. I asked her what was wrong, but she only shook her head. I pulled her into me so that I could peek at her back. She resisted, but I was much stronger. Imagine my surprise when I saw enough welts on her back to give Kunta Kinte a run for his money. To say that I was enraged would have been an understatement.

Shorty didn't deserve this bullshit for real. I didn't know how much longer I was going to be able to sit back in silence. She knew I was pissed to the max. She attempted to distract me by planting soft kisses on my neck and earlobes. I only went with the flow because I knew she didn't want to discuss the bullshit right now. I asked her to remove her bra, since I was afraid of hurting her again.

My mouth watered as her perky breasts sprang into view. I instantly begin to suck on them muthafuckas before she could change her mind. Women were indecisive like that sometimes. They knew damn well that they wanted the D as much, if not more than we wanted their little twats. As I suckled on one of her pretty ass tits, I glanced up at her and watched as her mouth formed a perfect O.

Her eyes rolled to the back of her head before she threw her head back. I heard her whimpering and moaning my name. This shit had my dick rocked the fuck up. I had to set my man free, even if I wasn't going to get any pussy tonight. I felt her body stiffen when she heard my zipper.

"Relax baby girl, I'm not going to hurt your little ass. You just got my dick hard as fuck and the shit is hurting in my jeans. *He* needs to breathe for a minute until he goes back to sleep," I reassured her.

She briskly glanced back and forth between my face and my dick with wide eyes. She was making me dizzy with that shit.

Yeah, a nigga was blessed in the dick department. We both watched as pre-cum oozed from the tip of my dick.

"Cee Cee, have you ever touched one before?" I asked with low eyes already knowing the answer to my question.

She hurriedly shook her head no. I grabbed her hand and started sucking on her small fingers. I then popped her right nipple back into my waiting mouth. I still had the hand that I had been sucking on. I took that hand and placed it on my chest. Her respirations hastened and she tried to remove her hand from my grasp.

I kept it in a firm grip as I continued to slide her hand from my chest to my toned abdomen. Finally landing on my engorged dick, I opened her hand and wrapped it around my meaty pipe. I then assisted her in stroking my ten-inch dick. My shit was so thick that her small hand couldn't fit around the entire circumference of my throbbing wood.

I had sniffed a little coke prior to picking shorty up so my sexual senses were heightened like a muthafucka. Truthfully, her hand game was feeling better than some of the pussy I had been tapping lately. Enjoying the feeling, I started thrusting upward into lil mama's hand as if I were beating a pussy up.

My suction on her erect nipple also became firmer, causing Cee Cee to yelp, "Oh fuck! Ummmm.......Eli!"

The way she moaned my name was so sexy to me. The next thing I knew, I was nutting all over shorty's hand. She glared at me as if I had just shit on her or something.

"Ewwww Eli! Get this shit off of meeeeeeee! Get it off!" She dramatically whined.

Had she had a knife at that moment, she probably would have chopped her damn hand off. I grabbed her head and delicately kissed her on her forehead before casually reaching for the wipes and hand sanitizer that I kept in my glove compartment. She silently wiped her hand off and discarded the used wipes out of the window. She then squirted a copious amount of hand sanitizer onto her hand before placing the items back into the glove compartment.

I smiled at her innocent ass and decided to leave her alone for the night. Hell, I had just busted a big ass nut all over her pretty little hand. I was satiated for now. I pulled her into me so that we could catch the last thirty minutes of the movie. Yeah, Cee Cee didn't know it yet, but her ass was mine. She had me going against my own codes. She had me out here kissing and shit. It was almost time for her big surprise.

"Thanks for that Ali," I teased, while taking her hand into mine.

« Chapter 13 Genetics »

The Past "Mike"

THE MOMENT OLE GIRL tapped me on my shoulder, and I saw Cee Cee grilling us, I knew I was fucked. Believe it or not, I loved my girl. Alicia was damn near perfect, definitely wifey material. She was beautiful, intelligent, she was thick, could dress her ass off and I knew she wasn't with a nigga for money. She was with me beforehand, besides; her mom was no slouch in the finance department.

I had always had a difficult time staying faithful in relationships. I think the shit was genetic. All of the men in my family were hoes. Why settle for fucking the same old pussy when there were so many different varieties out there? Don't get me wrong, Alicia's pussy was probably the best shit that I have ever had grip my dick. I loved her pussy even more because I was the only nigga walking this Earth that knew what that shit felt like. She was my bitch. I owned her and that pussy. I would never leave her ass or allow her to leave me.

My only issue with Alicia was she wasn't freaky enough. She was scared to suck my dick and I couldn't fuck the dog shit out of her the way that I wanted to. She always fought the dick and screamed that it hurt. I loved fucking her doggy style so that I could watch her fat ass jiggle and see my dick being swallowed whole by her pussy. She would only allow it on special occasions. She always wanted plain and boring missionary style sex.

I have been unintentionally fucking around on Alicia from day one. After I popped that cherry, I had spent an entire week with my ex. Honestly, I didn't want to. I wanted to be a better man for Alicia because I knew she deserved better. The day after I deflowered my baby, I received an urgent call from my ex, Tamar, informing me that she was pregnant with my baby. She stated that she would abort the baby if I paid for it and spent a few days with her prior to and following the abortion.

Like I said, I didn't want to go, however, what other choices did I have? I figured a little money, time and dick were a small price to pay to get rid of her and our little problem. I damn sure wasn't ready for any snot nosed kids. I had goals and nothing or no one was going to stop me from obtaining them. I knew that by the time my little week with Tamar concluded, I was going to have a lot of explaining to do. I had felt so guilty about the entire ordeal that I opted to ignore my pager and phone that week.

When I finally worked up the nerve to call her, it nearly broke my heart to hear her crying on the other end. I hated when she cried, especially when I was the cause of her unhappiness. She thought that I had only wanted to hit it and quit it. That shit couldn't have been further from the truth. I had never loved any woman the way that I loved Alicia. I couldn't really come up with any reasonable excuses for my week-long absence.

I'd concocted an elaborate story about my grandfather dying. The truth was my grandfather was alive and well. He lived a few blocks away from us. I hated to lie on my OG, but a nigga was desperate. I didn't want to lose my shorty...especially after only sexing her one time. I needed more. A lot more. I wasn't giving that freshly broken in pussy away to anyone. I understand that I am selfish as fuck. However, I couldn't have cared less. I wanted my cake and you better believe that I was going to eat that shit too.

I have been fucking around on her with too many women to count, but the thought of some other nigga in between her thighs enraged me. My extra curricula activities didn't affect us. I always strapped up. Well except for with Alicia and Tamar. I never ate stray hoes out and I damn sure wasn't about to have any illegitimate bastards popping up out of nowhere. I had taken care of my one little scare. I never brought any drama around Alicia. I let these bitches know upfront that they needed to stay in their lanes.

They were all informed that I would never leave Alicia for any of them. Unfortunately, I did have to fuck a few bitches up that caught feelings and got out of line. Apparently, that was another trait that ran in my family. The men didn't hesitate to put their women in check by *any* means necessary. I know I sound like a punk, but I didn't have any qualms about putting my hands on any bitch or nigga that deserved it.

I treated my girl like the beautiful queen that she was. I was always respectful in her presence. I had never laid a hand on her either. She knew how to obey me. These other broads needed to take notes. I did want to fuck Cee Cee up in that restaurant that day. If she hadn't been with Eli's ass, I probably would have murked the bitch just to keep my secret...*a secret*. I couldn't stand that nosey ass bitch.

I don't think she ever liked me for her friend, but she tolerated me. A smile spread across my face as I envisioned Celeste's snooty ass eating the lasagna that was marinated with my semen. She deserved every salty seed that slid down her hungry throat. I could tell she didn't buy my dead grandpa story back then, but thankfully, she never pushed the issue with Alicia.

Because I couldn't fuck Cee Cee up at The Melting Pot, you better believe that hoe Sha'Keisha felt my wrath that night. If her bitch ass hadn't been tempting me with her new tongue piercing, I wouldn't have gotten caught up. Because of her sociable pussy, I was now at risk of losing the love of my life. As soon as Sha'Keisha sat her ugly ass in my car, she knew what it was.

I was tempted to make the skeezer walk home, however, I wanted some neck first. She and I had been fucking around for a while, so she knew how I got down. These stupid bitches loved getting their asses beat...why else would she keep crawling back to a real nigga?

Once the car doors closed, she tried to crack a joke. Before I knew it, I had two pieced the comical bitch in the face.

"Laugh at that, bitch! You better go to church and pray like hell that my girl is in a forgiving mood and doesn't leave me. If my baby walks away from me, I'm going to kill you and her ass!" I growled as spittle flew from my mouth, landing on her face.

My fists connected with her face after every three to four words I spewed. Finally, I stopped the attack once I noticed her bottom lip split.

"Aye bitch, I'm still hungry. I'm going to a Wendy's drive thru. I'll ask them for some ice for your fucked-up face. Then we will head back to your place because I still want some of that wet-wet. Busted lip or not you will be giving a nigga some dome tonight," I advised her cry baby ass.

She was even more hideous once she started crying. Why did I even bother with this hoe?! Flashbacks of her sucking on my balls from the back quickly refreshed my memory.

"Sha'Keisha, I swear to God you better not be looking like that once I start eating. If you cause me to lose my appetite, I will kill you bitch. You hear me? Fix that ugly ass face of yours!" I barked.

Her tears quickly came to a halt. All I heard out of her were some occasional sniffles. I just loved an obedient bitch. I couldn't believe that I may lose my girl over this troll sitting next to me. I would be placed in the Guinness Book of World Records as the dumbest nigga on the planet. Below my mugshot would be my story along with comparison pictures of Sha'Keisha and Alicia side by side.

I busted out laughing at my own crazy ass thoughts. I noticed Sha'Keisha peeking at me with her one good eye probably wondering if I had finally lost my damn mind.

"Bitch, take yo *eye* off me and look into yo lap or something," I spat.

Man, this muthafucka was lucky she was a freak! Once we reached Sha'Keisha's place, I noticed that Alicia had paged me. I rushed into Sha'Keisha's house and used her landline. I made sure to block the number.

"Hello," I said.

"Hey baby! I've missed you so much baby!!!" Alicia gushed.

"Is that right? Baby I miss yo sexy ass too. I love you, boo."

"How long are you going to be on punishment daddy? And why is your number not showing up?"

"Alicia, I'm on my way over there now. We really need to talk about something. Is your mom home?" I inquired.

"Okay...is something wrong? No, she is working tonight."

"Just wait up, I am coming over."

"Alright handsome. I will wait up for you. I love you, be careful."

By the time we ended our call, I wasn't even interested in fucking Sha'Keisha's ass. Her face had nearly doubled in size and I knew that I would have to kill her for not topping me off properly. I'd give her ass a pass tonight because I just wasn't feeling it. I tossed a few crumpled bills at her from my pocket and kept it pushing.

After all, it was the hoe's birthday. That is the only reason she didn't get a Jr bacon cheeseburger to begin with. She fucked with ya boy heavy and that's why I had originally decided to bless her with such an expensive meal. My conscience was fucking with me and I was feeling guilty as hell. I needed to go ahead and get this dreaded conversation over with. I knew if I didn't own up to this shit that Cee Cee's little midget ass would have no problem with filling her in.

I wanted to be the first to break this shit to Alicia. I owed it to her. I also needed to tell her *my* version of events because I'm sure they differed from Cee Cee's version, just a tad bit. I was a victim too in all of this. Fuck! Why did Cee Cee and Eli have to be there today of all damn days? Eli made me sick just sitting there as if his shit didn't stink. Oh, I knew all about that pretty muthafuckas bet.

We were not boys per se, but we did kick it with the same crowds seeing how we were both extremely active in the school sports. Word on the street was that his ass placed a thousand-dollar wager for Cee Cee's cherry. I was about to put that ass on blast until he shot me the look of death.

I'm no punk by a long shot, but I know this nigga was a force to be reckoned with. He was single-handedly responsible for a lot of the missing posters displayed around town. I knew when to pick my battles. You better believe that nigga would get his sooner...rather than later.

« Chapter 14 Woman's Intuition »

The Past "Alicia"

AS I SAT ON THE toilet, I dreaded peeking at the fourth test that I was sure would yield the same results as the first three. How could I have been so irresponsible? Mike and I never used protection. Whenever I would beg him to use a condom he would get upset and accuse me of cheating on him.

He would give me the same old speech, 'Baby that is my pussy. I don't want to feel no damn plastic. My dick can't even get hard when I put them muthafuckas on. Besides, they're too fucking tight. I want your sweet warm juices dripping all over my bare dick. You know I got you. I will pull out before I bust off.'

Sadly, he rarely remembered to pull out before he 'busted off.' I was afraid to go on birth control pills because I feared a lot of their side effects and I did not want my mother finding them. I couldn't believe that I was sixteen and pregnant. I would've ended up on one of those damn reality shows...had they existed back then.

My mom was extremely cool and understanding, but I really didn't want to ever disappoint and embarrass her in this way. I knew this revelation would forever change the way she looked at me. I hadn't even told her that I was out here sexing. She is no dummy, so I knew she had her suspicions; however, she had never confronted me about it. She knew that Mike and I had been getting closer over the past year.

Mike was overall a good guy. He treated me well and I truly believed that he loved me. Lately I have been feeling as if he's been brushing me off, but I'm not quite sure why. He was my first love and I loved his ass to pieces. I wanted to marry him one day and I wanted him to father all of my babies...just not so soon. My goal was to finish high school first. I wanted a career and to be established before starting a family.

I wanted to join the Army and serve my country just as my late stepfather had. He was such an inspiration. There were many benefits to joining the military, yet the biggest one for me was the paid education. I had decided that I also wanted to follow in my mother's footsteps and become a nurse. I figured I'd just kill two birds with one stone. Plus, my body would be even more on point from the rigorous training.

I had been experiencing severe morning sickness. My period was over a month late and my breasts were so tender lately. I always kept track of all my cycles because I have been trying to avoid having sex during my ovulatory windows. I knew it wasn't foolproof, but so far, we had been extremely lucky. The thing about Mike was he loved my pussy.

After sex, he'd often have me sleep in a way that would allow his dick to remain inside of me at all times. If it slipped out, he'd wake up immediately to reinsert himself. My boo was crazy like that, but I wouldn't have it any other way. I had planned on revealing my pregnancy to him tonight during our date. However, he had called me and informed me that he couldn't make it due to him being punishment.

This was news to me because Mike was an intelligent jock. He always performed well in school effortlessly. I had no reason to doubt what he was telling me, so I just moped around the house. I had truly been missing my man lately. I tried not to be too clingy and allowed him to breathe. I was happy that Cee Cee had finally decided to start dating. I didn't think that my girl was ever going to get to first base with her crazy ass parents. Eli was sexy as hell and he was definitely on boss status.

Call it women's intuition, but for some reason my baby was all I could think about lately. I didn't know if this pregnancy had me missing his ass like this or if something were amiss. I decided to page him after fighting with my conflicted emotions. He called back right away as always and told me we needed to talk. He stated that he was on his way.

In a flash, I had hopped in and out of the shower...just in case he decided he wanted to do more than just talk. I threw on an orange tank top with matching boy shorts. My tantalizing ass cheeks were spilling out of the bottoms. With it being a Friday night, the twins were spending time with their paternal grandparents. It was going to be just me and my baby tonight.

He called me again from a payphone, asking if I needed anything before he arrived.

I was craving chicken so I replied in one breath, "Can you please stop by Popeye's Chicken? I want a two-piece white, make it spicy with a regular fry. Oh, and a large sweet tea without ice. I need a few packets of honey as well. I love you, bae! Thank you!"

"I don't know why you bothered saying all that shit. You order the same exact thing every time. You know I got you, beautiful. I'll be there in a minute," he replied.

I smiled and thought about how lucky I was to have someone like Mike in my life. I knew that he was going to make the perfect husband one day. I played some slow music and lit some candles in my bedroom. I then heard a soft knock on the front door. I opened the door and my baby rushed me.

He pulled me into his arms and kissed me as if his life depended on it. I loved that about him. He was the same no matter who was around. He was extremely affectionate towards me in all settings. He smiled brightly and told me how great I smelled and how much he'd missed me. We sat down at the dining room table and he watched me closely as I ate.

"You know that I love you, right? I mean really really love you. I would ask you for a kiss, but I'm afraid your greedy ass will bite my lip off," he chuckled before continuing.

"Naw, but seriously bae, I am going to marry you one day and give you the world. When I make it to the NBA, we will have the world eating out of the palms of our hands." He genuinely exclaimed.

I stopped chewing long enough to acknowledge that I knew he loved me.

He continued, "Before you hear it from anyone else, I wanted to be the first person to tell you that I had taken Sha'Keisha out to eat this evening. She was supposed to help me study and as payment, I decided to treat her to dinner. Well anyway, I had forgotten my books at the crib. By the time I realized it, I just decided to head on over to The Melting Pot to meet Sha'Keisha. Plus, it was her birthday.

See the thing is, I ran into Cee Cee and Eli there. Cee Cee of course thought something was going on that wasn't. I told them it was all a huge misunderstanding. They were informed that I was going to head straight over here and clear things up. I have never cheated on you and don't even find that girl attractive. It was strictly platonic." He rambled on breathlessly.

My heart fell into the pit of my stomach because I knew he was lying to me. Not only did this story sound like bullshit, he couldn't even maintain eye contact with me. I had a feeling that his ass had something going on...I just didn't know what. I couldn't believe that my man was cheating on me and with that homey the clown looking bitch of all people. As soon as her name dripped from his cheating ass lips, I already knew what time it was.

No nigga worth their weight in gold fucked with her ass unless some head or pussy was involved. I had classes with that hoe, and she was dumb as a box of rocks. If she was his solution to improving his grades, then he was in a world of trouble. Then this asshole had the audacity to tell me that he "forgot the books." Who in the fuck did he think he was dealing with?! My momma didn't raise a fool.

"Shut the fuck up Mike!" I finally interjected cutting his bullshit short.

"You must think I'm a muthafucking fool. I warned your ass that if you ever cheated on me that it was a wrap. No negotiations and no excuses! I have been nothing but good to your ass and this is the thanks I get? Did you listen to that story as it escaped from your trifling ass lips?! You are foul as fuck Mike.

For the record, we are no longer together. I got all these niggas checking for me, but I am over here stuck on stupid and being faithful to your funky ass. Oh no, not after today! I am going to find me a nigga who respects and cherishes my ass. Lose my fucking number. If you see me in public don't even..." That was all I managed to get out before he started choking the hell out of me.

"Shut the fuck up Alicia! Shut up! You better not even *think* about another nigga as long as I'm alive. Bitch you belong to me. I told your ass that I didn't fuck that hoe. I wouldn't do that to you. Come on baby don't do this! I'm not going to let you leave me over some shit I didn't even do. Hell, I could have fucked, but I didn't. I didn't even want to. Maybe I should have since you are accusing me anyway. Bae, I only have eyes for you. The only thing I am guilty of is treating the hoe to dinner for her birthday...for that a nigga is sorry! Please forgive me?!" He pleaded.

By this time, he had completely loosened his grip from around my neck. My neck was killing me, and I knew it had to be red as hell. I had never known Mike to behave this way and I was genuinely scared. Normally I could hold my own with most people, but he could kill my ass right now and no one would even know he had stopped by. I decided to play it smart, but honestly, I had to let him know that we were truly over.

By this time, we were both crying. How could I be so in love with this guy just thirty minutes ago and want to blow his fucking head off now? He repulsed me and I wanted him out of my sight...out of my life! I was not one of those weak ass bitches that forgave shit like this. I knew my worth and this nigga was not about to have me lowering my standards to accommodate his shortcomings. I was a bad bitch and this nigga was replaceable.

He had violated miserably. First, he cheats on me and then has the nerve to put his hands on me. I couldn't wait to get Cee Cee's side of the story. Through his tears, he reached for me. He tried to kiss my lips. I turned my nose up at him as if he smelled like a pot of old 'chitlins' on a hot summer day. He then decided to stand in front of me with his weak ass apologies.

When he noticed that his pleas and kisses were falling on deaf ears, he kneeled down and attempted to pull my boy shorts to the side so that he could eat me out. Normally, I would have gladly spread eagle and rode the fuck out of his skilled tongue...but today was different. Things would never be the same. I slapped him in his face and told him to keep his fucking hands off me.

"I meant every fucking thing that I said Mike. You standing in here choking me out is not going to cloud my judgement and make me want to stay with you. In fact, quite the contrary, you punk. I fucking hate you! Get the fuck out!!!" I spat venomously.

His big ass flinched as if my words literally stung him.

"You know what Alicia, you are really trying to get me to fuck you up tonight. I understand that you're upset, and you need a little time to process everything. Neither of us are leaving this relationship. The sooner you realize that, the better. Just remember that shit. Let me take a piss and I will leave you alone for the night. I will be calling you tomorrow and I expect you to answer bae."

He disappeared into the bathroom and I broke into a fit of uncontrollable sobs. I was hurting so badly on the inside that I thought I was going to die. I felt dead. Empty. How could he do this to me? How could he? I was so engrossed in my own thoughts that I didn't even notice him walk back into the living room.

"Do you have something you want to tell me Alicia?" He asked wearing a smile so huge it reached his eyes.

Shit! I had forgotten to get rid of those damn pregnancy tests. Truth be told, in the mist of all this chaos, I had even forgotten that I was pregnant. I guess I should've been happy that he had found them instead of my mother tomorrow morning.

"That was why I wanted us to go out tonight, Mike. I wanted to tell you that we were having a baby. None of that shit even matters now because I am damn sure not keeping anything associated with your cheating, abusive ass. I'm having this little muthafucka vacuumed out of me as soon as I can squeeze in an appointment. Anyway, you were leaving, right?" I retorted.

"You fucking bit..." He was quickly interrupted as he lunged at me.

Thankfully Cee Cee and Eli had just come home. I was convinced that I saw murder in his eyes. How hadn't I picked up on his dark side before? The man that I thought I loved was the devil. I saw it in his eyes as my best friend and Eli approach us. I wanted him out now.

"This shit is not over Alicia. I swear if you abort my seed or if I catch you around another nigga I will murk his ass...and then come for you. I mean every fucking word too. I love you, bae. If I cannot have you, you better believe that no one else will," he coolly whispered.

He roughly kissed my forehead. I watched him slide the pregnancy tests into his pocket, before storming out of the door. He didn't even bother closing it with his stupid ass. I really did hate his ass. I couldn't wait until Monday morning so that I could schedule that fucking appointment!

« Chapter 15 Reincarnation »

The Past "Gladys"

I HOPE EVERYONE UNDERSTANDS that I love my daughter more than life itself. Sadly, I loved my husband more. You must know the entire story before you prejudge me. I did not like ninety-five percent of the things that took place in my home. Together we have endured unimaginable things. You see when I met my husband, he was not living right. He was eight years older than me. I had always seen Lukas around the neighborhood engaging in various illegal activities from gambling to slinging that dope around.

At one time, he had even dabbled a little in the pimping business. Although Lukas was much older than I was, it was hard not to notice how handsome he was. He never knew his father, but was under the impression that he was some Cuban trick. He was not a large man; however, he had a powerful presence.

A gorgeous woman was always on his arm. Deep down I would feel a tinge of jealousy, although I never knew why. He was too old for me and I knew he was way out of my league. Don't get me wrong, I was cute and all, but not glamorous like those models that always flocked around him.

I would notice him watching me at times though. His eyes would linger on me for a second or two longer than socially acceptable, before he would continue on with his business. I was well aware that he was a force to be reckoned with and he was feared by many. My husband could be ruthless.

I on the other hand was raised by my dad, after my mother passed away while giving birth to me. Sometimes we receive ominous signs that we unfortunately fail to take heed to. My mother had battled with fertility issues until the very end. Prior to becoming pregnant with me she had suffered through one botched teenage abortion, two miscarriages and one stillbirth.

You would think that she would've taken the hint and stopped trying to conceive. No, not my lovely, yet stubborn mother. She was determined to have a baby...despite the costs. My mother had apparently gotten pregnant by an older neighborhood boy when she was just thirteen. To spare the family from embarrassment, my grandmother promptly took her to get an abortion.

Receiving an abortion in the 1940's was an extremely dangerous deed...especially when performed in a neighbor's basement. My dad later told me that my mother had become septic and nearly died after this abortion. She had told my dad that she was forced to drink alcohol to numb the pain. She remembered a wire hanger being burned for sterility and the smell of rubbing alcohol permeating through the air. The pain from the procedure was so unbearable that she passed out.

She woke up days later in excruciating pain. She always believed that her baby woes were attributed to that abortion. Her doctors warned her that due to extensive uterine scarring coupled with a congenital heart condition, she was tap dancing into dangerous territories. Obviously, her pregnancy with me was very much welcome, yet extremely high risk.

She was on bedrest throughout her entire pregnancy. She made sure she took all of her prenatal vitamins faithfully. She also closely monitored her dietary intake. She was determined to finally become the mother she had always dreamt of being. My mom flat lined twice during my birth. Her heart was simply too weak to withstand the demands of child labor.

She never recovered after she went unresponsive the second time. Luckily, due to a quick-thinking obstetrician, I was cut from my dead mother's hemorrhaging body, in the nick of time. I'm sure the entire ordeal was bittersweet for my daddy. He had lost his beautiful wife, yet gained a daughter all within an instant. I was their miracle baby.

A real woman never divulges her true age; however, I will say that I strongly believe that had I been born today, my mother would have survived. There is very little doubt in my mind of that fact. There are so many wonderful screening and preventative tools out there today. The technology is out of this world nowadays. Also, in those days, African Americans had many restrictions...especially in regard to healthcare. No heroic measures were to be done to save a black woman in those days.

Today, my mom could have easily opted to go the surrogacy route. This alone would have spared her heart from the intolerable stress of childbirth. Huhhhh...I suppose there is no point in dwelling on the should'ves, could'ves, or the darn would'ves. My daddy had also been a teacher who taught in the inner city. He gave me a solid foundation and I had been brought up in the church.

My father taught me to respect myself and others. He also drilled it into my head that I was special and should keep my head in the books and away from the boys. My father preached that I should only marry the lawyer or doctor types. He cautioned me never to get caught up with any of the hoodlums around our way. I truly never intended to.

I prided myself on being a virgin at seventeen. Several of my friends had already had babies. My dad quickly nipped those friendships in the bud. My dad was not perfect, but I can honestly say he was an amazing father. He always made sure that I never went without. My father had been my protector. I often told myself that my future husband would have to be just like him.

Unfortunately, our lives do not always turn out as planned. My father had developed a heroin addiction shortly after I turned fifteen. I noticed a huge change in his character. For as long as I could remember, my dad would sometimes experience periods of extreme sadness. It was a sadness that I could never seem to reach or soothe. I've noticed him just staring off into space. I'd often wonder if he were thinking about my mother.

I pondered if he resented me and wished that she were here instead of me. He'd never said it and his actions never showed it. I just speculated. He was able to maintain his teaching position for as long as he could, but he was eventually terminated for absenteeism and his erratic behaviors.

Times were extremely tight. We were receiving late and disconnection notices daily. I was now taking care of my father for the first time. He truly did make several attempts to get clean, but the drug was always victorious against his will. I would never wish that addiction on my worst enemy. I had found a waitressing job, however it never seemed to be quite enough to keep up with the bills.

My only solace was the fact that my father had at least paid the house off in full. If he hadn't, we would've been tossed out on our rear ends long ago. There were many times when my father would go days without eating and bathing. I literally had to take care of those fundamental things for him. It tore me to pieces having to watch my father deteriorate before my eyes.

He had always been so vain and meticulous about his appearance. I owed him at least that much for taking care of me my entire life. On Christmas day, which also happened to be my eighteenth birthday, I had decided to run to the grocery store so that I could get some wings, frozen fries, cake mix, icing and ice cream. It was not the traditional Christmas/birthday feast, but it would have to do considering my meager budget.

I had picked up overtime just so that I could afford today's items. After leaving the grocery store, I took the bus to the mall since our car had been repossessed. I wanted to get this nice sweater I had seen for my dad as a Christmas gift. We were beyond broke, but I wanted to do something nice for him even if it were small.

I really felt like celebrating today. My dad had told me that after we celebrated, he was going to try an actual rehab facility this time. My dad had been contacted by his old job. He was assured that he would be given the opportunity to redeem himself. Of course, he would have to be clean and remain that way. He seemed so upbeat this morning before I'd left. I felt as though I was getting my father back.

"Baby girl, I am tired of living like this. You deserve so much more than this life I have forced you into. What type of role model have I been to you lately? You should be focusing on school, but you are constantly at my bedside playing nurse. You should be filling out college applications and worrying about which lipstick color to wear...not which bill is due.

I've let you down big time, but I'm determined to spend the rest of my life making it up to you. I miss teaching. I'm done with this. I love you and I hope that you don't hate me for turning into a junkie. Let's celebrate. Once you get back, I'm going to get better for the both of us. This time will be different Gladys," he tearfully beamed.

"Dad, I love you too. I could never hate you so don't ever say that. You are all I have. You have always been there for me whenever I've needed you...with no questions asked. I'm just happy that you're not trying to beat this demon alone this time. God will see you through," I choked out as I hugged him.

Who knew that was to be my very last conversation with my daddy?

Later that day, when I opened our front door, a feeling of dread consumed me. Nothing looked out of place; however, I was experiencing some serious piloerections as the hairs on the back of my neck stood at attention. I placed my bags on the kitchen table and slowly walked towards my father's room. I shakily called out to him, but was met with deafening silence. I did not see him, however, I noticed his suitcase lying on his bed. He appeared packed and ready to go.

I hesitantly continued into his bathroom and that's when I was met with the worst scene of my life. My beloved father was sprawled out on the bathroom floor covered in his own feces. It appeared that he had just taken a shower. His clean outfit was folded neatly on the counter next to the sink. A tourniquet was tied snugly around his left arm. An empty hypothermic needle was still hanging out of his arm.

His wide eyes stared blankly at the wall. He appeared to be shocked and full of questions even in death. I'm not sure if it was the smell of the excrement permeating the air or the sight of my father's nude dead body that caused me to upchuck everywhere. I had to get the hell out of there! I ran to the living room and dove onto the couch. I cried for what seemed like days, but in reality, it was probably about an hour or two.

"Hey beautiful, are you okay? You left your front door open and I heard you in here crying." Someone inquired.

I was too distraught to even acknowledge their presence. Additionally, they could have been a serial killer or rapist and I couldn't have cared less at that moment. I was on my period anyway, so if they were nasty enough to take it, heck they could have it!

"Gladys, right? Talk to me sweetheart. Why are you sitting in the dark crying?" The mystery person questioned while placing a comforting hand on my shoulder.

My vision was blurred by tears, so I wiped my eyes with my shirt. As he came into focus, imagine my surprise when I saw Lukas standing in front of me.

"Wha..what are you doing here?" I questioned.

"I'm cool with your pops. He called me earlier to tell me he was finally going to rehab. I am proud of him, for real. He asked me to drop him off after the two of you finished celebrating. Happy birthday...oh and um Merry Christmas too pretty lady. Is he ready?" Lukas inquired looking around.

"How do you know my father?" I quizzed, my voice barely audible.

"Me and Mr. Berry go wayyyyy back. Can you believe he used to be my teacher?! Wild, hunh? I heard about him getting hooked on that smack and reached out to him. I've been trying to get him help since I heard about this mess. He's a good dude. When he called me earlier asking for a ride to a rehab facility, I couldn't believe my ears. God is good, isn't he?"

He then asked again, "Is Mr. Berry here?"

Tears spilled from my eyes once again as I pointed a shaky finger towards his room. His brows rose as if to ask me what was going on. Thankfully, he took the initiative to walk to my dad's room. I was relieved because I could not utter the words, nor did I want to revisit the scene by escorting him back there. He rejoined me in the living room moments later with tears in his eyes.

I was touched that my father had greatly impacted his life as well. He shocked me by pulling me into a bear hug. My body stiffened, but after a few minutes I relaxed. I rested my head on his shoulder and wrapped my arms around him. We both sat there crying our eyes out. He then pulled away from me and asked me if I had a phone. I looked at him strangely and nodded yes.

I watched him pick the phone up and immediately realized he was calling 911. Why hadn't I thought of that? My poor father had been lying on that cold hardwood floor covered in poop while I've been sitting in here crying. I barely paid attention to Lukas's brief exchange with the dispatcher.

I was grateful that Lukas stayed by my side as I was questioned by several different people. That day was such a blur that I scarcely recall any names, faces or questions asked. I was so appreciative that Lukas had come into my life during such a rough patch. It was almost as if it were fate.

∞

Over the next few months he became a good friend. He was always a gentleman and even accompanied me to church most Sundays. That was always a big deal for my dad and me. What I liked most about him was that he had never made a pass at me. I didn't see the neighborhood terror that others claimed him to be.

Coincidentally, I turned eighteen on the day my father overdosed. I don't know what I would have done had I been placed into a foster home. My father had surprisingly managed to pay off his whole life insurance policy during his time as a teacher. That's just the type of man he was before his addiction took over. I almost hit the floor when they told me it was in the amount of one hundred and fifty thousand dollars. That was a lot of money in those days.

I used some of that money to give him a proper burial, paid my tithes to the church and was determined to put the rest into my savings account. The church was packed with hundreds of past students, fellow teachers and family members. He was undoubtedly loved. I was still working as a waitress, but was working more hours now.

I had also accumulated my fair share of regulars, so my monetary prospects were looking better. I often wondered if my dad had some secret savings account because, despite his addiction, my dad had never asked me for any money. He had never stolen from me either as I'd heard about other addicts doing to sustain their addiction.

I was occupying myself with work, school and filling out college applications. I had always wanted to be a teacher for as long as I could remember. I wanted to follow my father's path. He always had the most amazing stories to share at the dinner table. While he preferred to work with the older kids, I knew that I wanted to teach the younger kiddos.

I had always performed well in school. My father made sure of it. I was interested in a few colleges in state. I knew that with my GPA I could attend any university that tickled my fancy; however, I didn't want to venture off too far. It's not that I had any strong familial bonds there or anything. I just didn't want to leave the only home that I ever knew. I was so enthralled in my future and the loss of my father that I hadn't even thought about the senior prom.

I guess that was partially because none of the guys had asked. I was beautiful, but I was not sexy. My father closely monitored my clothing and everything that I wore had to be respectable. I dressed conservatively well. Guys my age were not interested in that. They wanted fast, loose women, so I was often passed up. That is until Nathan approached me at my locker one day.

Nathan was a tall lanky dark skin guy who was in several of my classes. He wasn't an ugly kid, he just really wasn't my type. I felt that he was a wannabe who tried way too hard to fit in, no matter the cost. He was the class clown who no one took seriously. When we were in elementary school, he had slipped me a note asking me to be his girlfriend. Of course, back then I considered boys as repulsive as a box filled with used tampons and turned him down with the quickness.

"Hey G, you are looking exceptionally pretty today. Did you do something different?" Nathan asked.

"No, I haven't changed a thing Nate. What can I do for you?" I asked skeptically.

"First, let me start off by saying I am sorry for your loss. I know how close you and Mr. Berry were. I know you don't take me seriously because I'm always around here joking, but on the real...I really like you G. I have been feeling you since we've been in pampers damn near.

You remember I wrote you that heartfelt note and you broke my little heart. You were my first crush girl! Soooo what I am asking you is...would you do me the honor of accompanying me to the senior prom? Don't break my heart again G." He begged while batting his lashes with his hands in the prayer position. He was flashing me a big Kool-Aid smile.

He was so darned goofy! My mind immediately drifted off

to Lukas and how I wished it were him asking me. My next thought went to how he was out doing him and probably viewed me as a little girl that he felt sorry for. Lastly, Nate had come to me so humbly that I just could not deny him. I wasn't sure if my father would have approved of this short-term union, but I was technically grown now. I needed to live a little.

"Remember we are going just as friends. I don't want you expecting nothing either and I mean it Nate," I warned him.

"Oh, the answer was yes, by the way," I added as I closed my locker and turned to him.

"You will not regret this G! I have your number so I will call you later today with the details," he excitedly bellowed.

He pecked my cheek as the bell rang alerting us that we were officially tardy.

∞

With prom just two short days away, I didn't have much time to get my little look together. I had decided on a soft pink ball gown. Its exaggerated flair made my already full hips stand out even more. The dress was covered with silver glitter and my ample bosom spilled over just enough.

I would have my long hair done in an up style that I had seen in a magazine last week. My heels were silver as was my clutch. It was the 70's and couldn't anyone tell me a thing! As I modeled in my gown, I heard a knock at the front door.

I noticed Lukas through the peep hole. I hastily flung the door open because I hadn't seen him all week. I was about to pull him into a hug when I noticed a strange expression on his face.

"Where are you going looking like Cinderella? Wow, you look stunning Gladys!" He asked with lust in his eyes.

"I was asked to prom and I was just trying on my dress. It fits perfectly. I didn't have to have any alterations made. That almost never happens," I filled him in.

Lukas was silent for a while before replying, "Who are you going to prom with? You must be careful out here. You know these horny clowns only want one thing."

"It's just Nathan from school. He is nice enough. He was the only guy who asked me, and I figured it would be fun. I will be careful," I promised.

"I guess it's okay. But listen, I can't stay. I just remembered that I have something to do. I will check on you soon, okay?" He stated.

"Seriously Lukas, you just got here. Stay for a while, I can whip us up something to eat quickly," I pouted.

"Naw, I'm good. Besides I'm sure your new little boyfriend wouldn't want you over here cooking for another man," he sneered before walking out of the door.

What the heck was his problem?! I waved his moody tail off and reunited with my mirror.

∞

Nate had truly outdone himself. He actually looked quite manly in his tuxedo. I was now able to appreciate how truly handsome he was. He had gotten his hair freshly cut. He had asked me if I wanted him to rent a limo, but I thought that was just too much. Plus, it is done so often that it wasn't even impressive to me.

He had opted to drive his own black Lincoln Town car. He gave me a corsage that matched my gown perfectly. I thought his little chinky eyes were going to pop out of his head once he saw me. He was smiling like he had won the Powerball. Everyone was looking on in amazement.

I received a lot of stares of course because many of the partygoers had never seen me dressed up like this before. I loved the attention and so did Nate. We danced, sang and joked as if we were the only two people in the room. I was amazed by all the fun we were having. Nate was enjoyable to be around. I had greatly miscalculated him.

After our prom queen and king were crowned, my feet had decided that it was time to go.

"Here you go Ms Pretty Lady. You've been in here working up a sweat. I figured you would be thirsty," he yelled over the music.

"Awww! You must've read my mind. I'm dehydrated over here," I replied fanning myself.

I quickly gulped down the punch, wishing he had brought over two cups. It was okay though, I had all the juice I needed at home. He grabbed my hand and we exited the party.

"Hey G, the night is still young. Do you want to swing by the park for a little while?" He asked.

"Nate, I'm sorry maybe some other time. My feet are killing me and I'm starting to feel sleepy suddenly," I answered.

"Come on, Gladys please!! Just for five minutes, I promise after that you can get rid of me. Everyone is supposed to be meeting out there and I just wanted to check it out before we head home. I don't want to look like a loser and go alone," he pleaded.

I just sat back, closed my eyes and nodded. "Only for five minutes Nate. I mean it," I whispered.

I felt him grab my hand and kiss it before driving off. I must have dozed off during the ride to the park because I woke up to Nate pulling down the front of my dress exposing my breasts. I thought I was dreaming at first until his mouth devoured my left nipple. I felt so weak and powerless at that moment. What on Earth was wrong with me? I weakly glanced around, but didn't see a soul in sight.

"Nate, please don't do this. I do not believe in sex before marriage. I don't want to have sex with you," I begged.

My cries fell on deaf ears. It was difficult for me to keep my eyes open, because I felt so drowsy. I was beginning to wonder if he had slipped something in that punch. He struggled a bit to get through all the layers of my dress. He had completely ripped my panties off. I watched as he stuck his middle finger into his mouth and then roughly pushed it inside of me.

I screamed out from the pain. He had incredibly long fingers. I watched as he removed his finger to suck it off several times only to reinsert it again. Tears were streaming down my face obviously because of the pain, but mostly because I hated being powerless. He rotated between sucking on my neck and breasts as I was forced to listen to my vagina make all types of gross noises as he continued fingering me. I was so humiliated.

"I knew that pussy was sweet Gladys. You thought I wasn't going to pay you back for embarrassing me in front of everyone back in the day? I didn't forget that shit. I'm about to take that shit out on this virgin pussy. You better hope that your ass can walk by the time I finish fucking you in all types of positions," he boasted.

"Seriously Nate, that happened in elementary school! We are grown now. Are you truly holding a grudge over that?! Come on, please don't do this. I am so sorry! I am sorry!" I begged as forcefully as I could.

All hope was lost as I watched Nathan begin to pull down his slacks. I turned my head because I didn't even want to see *it*. He had reclined my seat and was now hopping over to my side.

I continued to beg and apologize to deaf ears. Just as I felt the tip of his erection tap against my clitoris, I heard my door being snatched open. I watched as Nate was snatched out of his car by his neck.

"Get your stupid ass out of the fucking car Gladys!" I heard a familiar voice yell out.

"I…I…can't walk," I whispered.

"I think he slipped something in my drink. Please help me," I pleaded.

All was quiet except for the furious blows that I assumed were being delivered to Nathan's body. I fought desperately to keep my eyes open. I slowly turned my head and my eyes widened as I watched as Lukas pulled out a gun and emptied it into Nate's battered body. I didn't hear the shots, so I knew he had a silencer on his weapon.

Despite my sore, bloody vagina, I knew I was now safe. I smiled as I thought about how Lukas had once again saved the day. He had saved me from being brutally raped by that animal and for that I owed him my life! I was forever indebted to him. I couldn't help but wonder if he was my guardian angel. Perhaps my father had been reincarnated in the form of this beautiful being.

« Chapter 16 Severing Ties »

The Past "Celeste"

ELI AND I HAD BEEN growing closer by the day. I couldn't believe that I had actually jerked him off in his truck. I'm going to keep it real, I was pissed to the max when his ass nutted all over my hand. I couldn't wait to wipe that shit off me. I then wanted to slap the smirk off of his smug ass face. We'll just see if I ever do that nasty shit again!

I was so flattered when he had asked me to be his woman. The truth is, I was prepared to scream hell yeah until I noticed Mike's doggish ass in the restaurant. After catching him red handed cheating on my bestie, I was feeling a little distrustful of all men.

I had always felt that something was a little off with Mike, but I thought it was all in my head. He had always treated Alicia extremely well. I could tell that Eli was not happy about me telling him to allow me to think about it, but he would be okay. A day or two of consideration would not kill him. I wondered if he could actually be faithful. I had never heard of him being in an exclusive relationship before.

He'd be the first to admit to his womanizing ways. I didn't want to get played and end up just another notch on his incredibly long belt. I'd be lying to you if I said that I didn't want him in the worst way. My body reacts to him in ways I never knew were possible. I had to keep panty liners on deck because Ms. Kitty stayed dripping.

The way he was sucking on my neck and tits the other day had me ready to bust my pussy wide open for a real nigga! Honestly, I tried not to take it too far, because I didn't want him to see the freshly acquired welts on my back. The look in his eyes upon seeing them was one of pure fury.

I knew I had to distract his ass by any means necessary, before I ended up an instant orphan. Hence, my cum covered hand. Anyway, I know I probably should've reported my parents long ago...I just didn't have it in me. I would be eighteen and college bound soon enough.

You may be wondering what I had done to receive my painfully decorative back. Well my mom was snooping through my room and noticed some of the new outfits and thongs that I had purchased. Naturally she reported her findings to my father and he gladly beat me like I was a runaway in the movie Django. Those clothes were all cut up and their remains were promptly tossed into the trash.

Luckily for me, I kept most of my new clothes at Alicia's house anyway. So, it was only a minor setback to a major come up. School was going well. I had made all A's again. I was the number one student in all my classes and was still trying to figure out what colleges I should apply to next year.

I was still in love with my job as well. I had noticed that Joe was showering me with extra attention and was always staring at me from across the room. Yesterday he even "accidentally" brushed up against my ass four times as I worked the cash register. I just let it go. I didn't want to make a big to do out of nothing and risk losing my job.

I had just announced to everyone that I was going on my lunch break and asked Nivea to cover the register for me. I felt like eating Thai food and the food court came equipped with just about any cuisine you may crave. After receiving my food and grabbing a few napkins, I quickly took a seat at the closest table.

Only two bites into my meal, I heard, "Do you mind if I join you Celeste?"

I glanced up and noticed Joe gazing down at me. He laid a plate down that was holding two large slices of pepperoni pizza. He then followed suit as he sat in the chair next to me before I could even respond. I sarcastically motioned for him to go ahead and have a seat.

I was a little annoyed because this was my personal time. We both ate in silence for a few minutes. I really liked Joe, but lately some of his actions unnerved me. I just wanted a strictly professional work relationship with him. Not this weirdness he'd created between us.

"Celeste, I am sure you've noticed that I am quite fond of you. I know it is not appropriate, hell, my feelings for you aren't even legal yet. What I do know is that I have tried to ignore these thoughts and feelings, but they just won't go away," he rambled.

"Joe as you have already mentioned "we" would be wrong on so many levels. You have never mentioned it before, but I've noticed that you're wearing a wedding ring. You have a family that depends on you. You are way too old for me. I'm just a teenager who is still trying to find herself. Besides, I just started seeing someone. I like you Joe, but just not in that way. I'd like for us to keep things professional, okay?" I asked.

"You are absolutely right. Whoever this guy is that you're seeing is extremely lucky. I just wish that there were girls that looked like you back when I was in high school. I do have a family. Mia and I haven't been happy together in quite some time.

Don't get me wrong, I love her, but I am no longer *in* love with her. Our relationship has run its course. We decided about a year ago that we would have an open relationship. We are only staying together for the sake of our boys. I hear everything that you're saying, and I can only respect it. I will back off," He declared while throwing up his hands in surrender.

I smiled brightly and sighed in relief. I felt as if a huge weight had been lifted from me. I didn't think he would take it so well. I just knew I was about to be canned.

"Thank you so much for understanding Joe. I really appreciate everything. You have been so kind to me the entire time that I've been here. Well I guess my break is over. I should head on back before my boss fires me," I joked while dramatically checking the time on my watch.

I cleaned off the table and headed back to work.

The rest of the shift was uneventful. Eli was so considerate. He came all the way to my job to pick me up. He came early so I asked if he wanted to come in while I finished up. I introduced him to Nivea, Angelika, Tyra and Joe. I didn't miss the scowl that crept over Joe's face after the introductions were made.

He then quickly excused himself to the back. After finishing up, I left out with Eli. We were going to hang out at his house for the first time. I had asked my mother if I could go over to Alicia's for a little while to study for an upcoming exam. The truth is, I had already studied and felt more than prepared. That was just my cover so that Eli and I could spend some alone time together.

I had decided that I wanted to become his woman. I would tell him later on. It was about ten days since my birthday, and he kept bringing up having this big surprise for me. I wish he'd just give it to me already. Once we pulled up to Eli's house, I was quite impressed.

He did not live far, but his house was much bigger. It also looked as if it were recently built. His sister and brother were in the living room watching tv. I waved to them both after he formally introduced us. He stated that his grandmother always went to bed early so I would not get to meet her tonight.

He ordered several pizzas for all of us. We ate and joked while watching Martin. I absolutely loved that show. He then grabbed my hand and pulled me towards a door that appeared to lead to the basement. It was laid out down there. He had the basement set up like a large apartment.

He stated that while the house had five bedrooms upstairs, he wanted his privacy. I took a seat on the plush white couch while he surfed the tv for something to watch. I glanced down at my watch to make sure that it wasn't getting too late. I still had about an hour before I knew my parents would start looking for me, so I relaxed.

Eli looked at me seductively and flashed one of his infamous smiles. I blushed and looked down into my lap. Instead of sitting next to me on the couch, he kneeled in front of me on the carpeted floor.

"Cee Cee, I hope you don't think that I am one of these soft ass niggas, but I'm seriously feeling the fuck out of you, ma. I'm starting to fall for you baby. You are just so perfect to me. I have never brought another woman to the crib that I share with my family. You are definitely cut from a different cloth ma. Have you thought about what I asked you at the restaurant?" He genuinely inquired.

I was smiling from ear to ear. I couldn't believe that someone like him was feeling regular old me.

"I'm happy that our feelings seem to be mutual Eli. I have thought about what you asked me the other day and the answer is...yes. I don't want to get hurt. Promise me, if you ever decide that I am not what you want then you will let me know right away. Don't play with me and always keep it one hundred. I have never had a boyfriend before, but I will put forth a lot of effort into our relationship. I will do everything I can to make you happy. Just don't hurt me, okay?" I tearfully replied.

He kissed my hand and replied, "I could never hurt you Celeste. Boo, I love you. I only have eyes for you. I'm not going anywhere. Please believe that," he rebutted before tenderly kissing my lips.

I melted after he professed those three little words to me. All I had ever wanted was to be loved. In that moment, I knew that I too loved the man who had found it in his heart to love me even when my own parents didn't.

He then slipped me the tongue and he tasted so delicious. He then started nibbling on my ear lobes causing soft moans to escape my parted lips.

Suddenly he gazed up at me and asked, "Can I taste you? We don't have to do anything else if you don't want to. I just want to please my woman," he explained.

I nodded, but then I realized that I had on a panty liner as he started tugging at my pants. I was suddenly self-conscious because I hadn't showered since that morning prior to school and work.

"Eli I really want to do this, but do you think that I could take a quick shower? I've been going since this morning and do not feel the freshest at the moment. I just need about five minutes," I stated honestly.

"Of course, mi casa es tu casa baby. Come on and I will get you a towel and wash cloth," he offered.

I thanked him after amassing everything I needed to take a quick shower. The warm water was soothing. I took notice of how immaculate Eli kept his bathroom and I grew even more fond of him. As I stood in the shower, I kept asking myself if I were doing the right thing. Was I moving too fast? Would he think that I was a hoe? Would he brag to everyone tomorrow? Would my psychotic parents find out?

I must've changed my mind a few dozen times during my speedy shower. Thinking about how great it felt when Shawn 'tasted me' had my kitty purring and I decided to throw caution to the wind. Once I was satisfied with the freshness of all my 'hot spots,' I stepped out of the shower and dried off.

Since I didn't have a change of clothes, I decided to keep the towel wrapped around me. I exited the bathroom and didn't see Eli in the living room area where I had left him. I continued walking down the hall and found him lying on top of his bed. He grinned and waved me over. I slowly made my way over to his bed.

"Have a seat baby. I'm not going to bite."

"Ummm, bae you have something white on your upper lip, near your nose," I reported as I wiped it off.

He quickly examined his face in the mirror attached to his headboard.

"That damn baby powder got all over me when I sprinkled some on the bed. I didn't make my bed earlier and decided to freshen it up while you were in the shower. I think you got it all off me now. Thanks for saving me boo!" He jokingly elaborated while pulling me into a bear hug.

I giggled as he laid me onto the bed and started tickling me as if I were a toddler. I was laughing so hard that I had tears streaming down my cheeks. I mushed him in his head and told him that I wasn't going to let him taste me now since he tickled me without mercy.

"Cee Cee, come on now. You know I was just playing. Don't do me like that. I apologize for tickling you baby. I know we just ate, but I am craving *her* now," he replied massaging my pussy through my towel.

"I guess I'll forgive you this time...just don't let it happen again," I teased.

He reached for my towel, but I stopped him.

"Can you turn off the lights, please? I don't want you looking at my nakedness," I stated seriously.

He shook his head in disbelief as he went to turn off the light. After the lights were off, I removed the towel and hurriedly climbed under the covers.

"Tell me what you want me to do Cee Cee."

"You *already* know what I want you to do. Why are you playing with me boy?"

"I want you to be specific and tell me."

"You get on my nerves!"

"I'm listening. Tell me."

"Fine! I want you to eat my pussy! Happy now?!" I bashfully whispered feeling put on the spot.

"Now that wasn't hard, was it? As promised, your wish is my command, Ali."

He started with my nipples. He expertly swirled his tongue in circles making them harden more and more by the second. I grabbed a hold of the back of his head as he slurped away. He made sure to show the girls equal amounts of attention before slithering his tongue down to my freshly manicured toes. He snaked his tongue in between each of my toes causing me to catch my breath. I was whimpering and grabbing at the sheets in pure ecstasy. Eli smiled as he began to kiss and lick on my inner thighs.

He was intentionally teasing me, and it was driving me insane. When the tip of his moist tongue connected with my fleshy nether folds, I instantly cried out. This sensation was even better than I had remembered. He feasted on my sweet juice box as if this were to be his last meal.

He took my throbbing clit into his mouth and suckled on it as if it were a miniature dick. I arched my back and clamped my thighs tightly around his head. I didn't know how his ass was able to breathe. However, at that moment frankly, I did not give a damn.

"Ummmm suck on that wet pussy baby! That's it, right there. Oh fuck! Oooh......my God! I love that damn tongue of yours! Sssssssssssss!!!" I hissed.

When he grabbed me by the ankles like an infant having their diaper changed, I almost lost it when I felt his scorching tongue draw circles around my asshole.

"Eli, you are a nasty bastard, aren't you? Ooooo lick my ass!" I panted.

I felt like a possessed woman with very little control over my actions or words. Once he made his way back to my pussy and his lips begin to apply suction to my clit, a familiar sensation returned.

"Oh no! Not this shit again! Eli get up, I have to peeeeeeee!" I shrieked.

Unlike Shawn, he continued sucking, licking, slurping and humming on my clit.

"Did you hear me?! Your nasty ass must want a pissy mouth. I'm about to pee, baby move!" I said pushing on his head.

"Chill ma, lay yo crazy ass down. Yo ass is not about to pee. You're about to bust a big ass nut for a real nigga. Now let me do what I do."

"I sure hope you're right baby."

With that he went back to work. I silently prayed that I wouldn't give him a golden shower as I tried to get back into my zone. I felt Eli insert a finger into my tight dripping hole. The sensation became stronger and stronger as he dipped his tongue in and out of my vaginal folds.

I was chanting his name repeatedly. I started clawing at the back of his head while grinding the hell out of his face. My breathing increased as my legs begin to take on a mind of their own as they shook uncontrollably.

My eyes rolled to the back of my head as I screamed, "Unnnhhh God Eli...I think it's happening!!! Oh...my...God it feels sooooo damn good! Fuck...fuck...fuck!!!" I chanted as I felt a wave of euphoria wash over me.

I bit my bottom lip in an attempt to stifle some of my cries of pleasure. I watched him attempt to capture the gush of fluid that had escaped from my center.

Tears spilled from my eyes because I didn't know how else to deal with the fireworks that he had just ignited inside of my body. As I continued on my orgasmic high, Eli finally came up for air and kissed me on my lips. He was so alluring. Damn that boy was too fine! I could clearly see that his little man was rocked up.

"Cee Cee, do you think you're ready to go all the way? I know I said that I only wanted to taste you and I meant it when I said it...but you turned me on like a muthafucka. The way you were moaning a niggas name was driving me up a wall. I will understand if you aren't ready, but the kid just had to ask. I love you and don't want you to do anything that you aren't ready for," he stated looking so damn sexy.

Did he just really say that he loved me again?! Pure lust oozed from his eyes. I honestly wasn't 100% sure if I was ready or not. However, it was hard for me to say no when I was feeling so blissful. At that moment, I would've been down to rob a bank with his ass, had he asked.

"I guess we can do it as long as it doesn't hurt and you don't get me pregnant," I mumbled breathlessly.

He kissed my lips before going over to his nightstand to retrieve a condom. I anxiously watched as he began to take off his clothing. He slid the condom down the length of his shaft. Once his full length came into focus, the reality of it all hit me for the first time. Ms. Kitty instantly became drier than the Sahara Desert. I didn't want to do this, but I didn't have the heart to tell him as much. I just prayed that it didn't hurt too badly.

Maybe I was just overreacting, and it wouldn't be so bad after all. If it was terrible, why would women continue to do it? I was shaking like a leaf with my eyes clinched tightly as he made his way onto the bed. He climbed on top of me parting my legs with his knees. I felt his thick dick bobbing against my pussy as he kissed me.

"Damn Cee Cee, why are you shaking like that? Are you scared? Are you sure you're okay with this because we can stop," he stated.

"I...I'm sure...I think. Just stick it in," I stammered.

My eyes were still shut tightly, however, I could feel him peering down at me for a few moments. Then I felt the bed shift as he got up. My eyes flew open and I wore a puzzled expression on my face.

"What's wrong Eli? Did I do something wrong?" I panicked.

"No baby, you didn't do anything wrong. I just can't do it. Not tonight. Not like this. You deserve better for your first time. Come on and get dressed so that I can take you home before your parents put out an APB for yo little sexy ass," he joked.

"Thank you, Eli. You have really proven a lot to me tonight. I'm so happy that you came into my life baby," I replied.

∞

The next day I took the day off from school and work. I hardly ever missed because I enjoyed the escape from home. I knew once my report card came, I would have to explain my absence, but I would just have to cross that road at a later date.

Alicia had revealed to me that she was pregnant the same night we discovered Mike dining with the platypus.

She told me about their conversation and how he had told only half truths. I told her about the entire encounter. I then allowed her to listen to the voice recording. I hated to spring all of that on her especially after finding out about her pregnancy. She told me about Mike choking her out and how she was truly afraid of him.

Although I did not agree with her decision, I completely understood her when she expressed her desire to terminate her pregnancy. I would support my bestie regardless. I stated my opinion about it and moved on. Who was I to judge? I cannot say with absolute certainty that I wouldn't do the same thing if put in her position.

She had opted not to tell her mother about the baby since she had no plans of seeing the pregnancy through. She asked me to be her 'person.' She wanted me to drive her to the clinic where the abortion was to be completed. My stomach was in knots and I was silently praying that she would have a change of heart.

There were two other young women in the waiting area. One was accompanied by an older woman while the other sat next to a guy who appeared to be our age. I couldn't help but to wonder if they were there for the same reason.

It was at that moment that I was happy that I hadn't had sex with Eli last night. I was certainly not prepared to deal with those issues. I wasn't even sure if I ever wanted children. Alicia was called back to an examination room while I waited for her in the lobby.

I prayed that all went well for my friend and hoped that she would be able to live with her decision. I browsed through various magazines and worked on some crossword puzzles. I wished that I'd brought a textbook or two so that I could get a head start on some of our assigned readings for school.

The nurse had explained that while the procedure itself only took about ten minutes since she was only in her first trimester, she would have a lot of paperwork to complete. They would also draw her labs, obtain a urine specimen and perform an ultrasound.

They would thoroughly explain the procedure to her and offer grief counseling. I knew that I would probably be there for a couple of hours, especially if she needed extra time in the recovery room. I placed my ear buds in my ears and powered on my portable CD player. I closed my eyes and rested my head against the wall behind me.

I must have been tired as hell because the next thing I remember is the nurse telling me that Alicia was all done and would be out soon. Once I saw Alicia, I wanted to burst into tears. My friend looked so fragile and incredibly sad. She was walking extremely slow and clutching her abdomen.

She had received prescription orders to pick up pain medication and a prophylactic antibiotic. She declined the birth control prescription out of fear of her mother finding them. During the ride to the pharmacy I occasionally glanced at her and noticed tears streaming down her face as she stared out of the window.

I gently grabbed her hand and squeezed it. I knew she wasn't up to talking about what had just taken place, so I just wanted to silently reassure her that I wasn't going anywhere. After we picked up her medications from the pharmacy, I took Alicia home so that she could get some much needed rest.

I had made her some homemade tacos, which was her

favorite. She really didn't have much of an appetite. Mike had been blowing up her pager and house phone. I truly admired my friend's strength. A lot of women just allowed men to continuously cheat on them and I just couldn't understand it for the life of me.

Alicia was an amazing young woman who knew her worth. She ignored all correspondence with Mike and had grown irritated that he refused to move on. He of course continued to apologize and beg like Keith Sweat via voicemail. Then the apologies would be replaced by fits of rage.

He would call her the most awful names and threatened to cause her harm if she didn't return his calls. He had flowers and candy delivered, all of which were promptly tossed into the trash. I cursed her ass out for that shit because I could've eaten the damn candy! She had yet to see him face to face and was dreading that inescapable reunion.

She told me how he blew up when she had threatened to have an abortion. Alicia would only tell Mike about the abortion when she absolutely had to, out of fear of his reaction. I thought she was overreacting and felt she should have just told his ass now. This way, she could help him move on faster. I figured he was clinging to the possibility of them getting back together because she was pregnant.

Once he realized that she had terminated the pregnancy, he would know that their only tie was now severed. I stayed and catered to my friend until the time that I would have typically gotten off from work. I then went home as if I had just left from a hard day at work. No one knew the wiser...

« Chapter 17 Taking one for the Team »

The Present "Autumn"

AFTER MY MOTHER'S FUNERAL, life had been fairly good to me. The only thing that would have made this unfortunate circumstance better was having Wintress here with me. We were lucky I suppose, our foster parents made arrangements for us to visit one another twice a week in public settings. I continued to throw out hints to Mrs. Douglas about fostering Wintress.

She assured me that she was doing everything that she could to have Wintress placed with us. She stated that Wintress's foster parents were resistant, because they were hoping to foster with the possibility of adopting. They had started to bond with Wintress and truly did not want to part with her. This annoyed the hell out of me because she was not theirs to keep.

I was grateful that they loved her and were treating her well, but she was my flesh and blood. We were all each other had in the world. I was finally settling into my new school. Major changes like this were never easy, but I made do the best way I could. The Douglas' made sure that Chris, Landon and I wanted for nothing. I had been picking up a little sign language so that I could better communicate with Landon.

I had grown to love those two boys as if they were my biological brothers and I know they loved me too. They were always following me around but I didn't mind. Mrs. Douglas was a sweetheart, but she was always extremely busy volunteering in the community. She truly did have a heart of gold. As busy as she was, she was adamant about always making our meals.

In her absence, she relied on Don a lot to watch over the three of us. I was perfectly capable, but she always felt that we needed supervision. I guess I had been living with the Douglas family for about four months when the unthinkable happened. I was lying on my bed doing some homework when I felt a presence. Someone was watching me.

Thinking it was one of the boys, I glanced up ready to chase them down for spying on me. Instead, I was met with the unfortunate sight of Don's humpty dumpty looking ass. I was not alarmed because he was just strange like that. He was always popping up in weird places and I had grown to ignore him. He was nice enough, just odd as fuck.

"Oh, hey Don, what's up?" I asked looking back down at my homework.

"Nothing much, I was just seeing if you needed anything," he replied.

"No, I'm okay. I'm just finishing up some homework before I go to bed. I know it's late, but I won't be up much longer," I assured him with an exaggerated yawn.

Not taking the hint, he stepped into my bedroom and closed the door behind him.

"Don, where is Mrs. Douglas? Why did you close the door?" I asked growing worried.

"Shut up you little bitch! Listen up and listen close. My mother took the boys to their sports. I know a way that I can get your little sister to move in with us," he claimed.

"Really, how Don? That would make me the happiest girl in the world! I'd give anything to have my sister move in with us," I naively gushed.

A sinister smirk spread over his fat oily face as he stepped forward.

"You coming here was no accident. I heard about what happened to your mom on the news. I knew her once upon a time. A good buddy of mine from the police department had photos of you and Wintress in your mother's file. I thought you were too beautiful to put into words. I had to pay a pretty penny to have him pull strings to get you out here.

Now listen, you can accept what I'm about to present to you and your life will only continue to get better. Or you can say no and life as you know it will cease to exist," he paused before continuing.

"I want you. By that I mean, I want you physically, sexually, emotionally and in any other way imaginable. I will not force myself on you. It will all be up to you. I know that I'm not what one would consider attractive; however, I never want to get that impression from you.

Hopefully you will grow to love me as a boyfriend of some sort. Know that once you agree to my terms that you will not date or have sexual relations with anyone else for as long as I should want you. With you being an older teenager, you will have a difficult time being placed. Look around you, life doesn't get much sweeter than this.

If you agree to my terms, there is nothing I will deny you. I am not the enemy here. Believe me when I say that we share a common interest in all this mayhem. My mom has been going about handling the Price family all wrong. Just as their name indicates, everyone has one. I have made them a very generous offer and they are prepared to take it in exchange for your sister.

I will pay it once you agree and make good on your end of the bargain. Please know that if you say no, I will have my mother ship you to one of the shittiest homes imaginable. I will tell her that I caught you stealing...and you know she absolutely hates thieves. So Autumn, what's it going to be?" He offered while licking his thin dry lips.

"Don, you are kind of like my big brother now, in a way...," I stated trying to get him to see that his proposal was all the way fucked up.

He cut me off by bellowing out a loud hearty laugh. He'd even managed to sneak in a snort or two. I grew particularly repulsed as I noticed the strings of spit that always seemed to hoover in the corners of his mouth.

He then seriously stated, "Autumn, cut the bullshit and stop stalling. We are not related. The only connection that you and I have will occur only when my dick is sliding in and out of that pussy."

"How long do I have to consider this? If I say yes, can we do what you're asking me after you get Wintress please?" I begged.

He shook his head, "No sweetie, it doesn't work like that. Even though I have the Prices on board, it could take up to a month or even longer for her to be placed with us due to all the legalities. I've already been waiting for this moment for months.

Do you know how many nights I have spent shooting off loads to your pictures or how many faceless sluts I have fucked imagining it was you? It is time. I need to know right here, right now," he declared with finality.

I sat there deep in thought for a few moments. I looked him over and couldn't fathom kissing him let alone giving him my most prized possession. What choices did I truly have? If I said no, he would see to it that I never saw Wintress again. Well at least not until I was old enough to seek her out and pray that she hadn't been adopted. He wouldn't hesitate to send me off to a crack house in the slums somewhere.

I looked around at the new life that I had been given and I didn't want to lose it. If I said yes, I would virtually become his sex slave. I allowed a single tear to violate my right cheek as I nodded my head. He smiled and rubbed his pudgy hands together as if preparing for the tastiest meal of his fat life.

"Let me make a few things clear. No one can know about our arrangement, especially my old lady. If you tell anyone, I will not hesitate to kill you. I have friends in high places that will help me dispose of your body with no questions asked. Remember, you are not to see other people. If you do, I will no longer desire you and I will ship you and your sister to different homes. Your body now belongs to me and you will do whatever I ask you to in the bedroom. Are we clear?"

I again nodded slowly, while avoiding eye contact.

"Come over here and kiss me," he demanded.

I stood up and unhurriedly walked over to him. We were the same height. As I stared at his lips, he again asked me to kiss him. His breath smelled horrible. How could someone possess so much money, yet couldn't pay to rid himself of his ferocious halitosis?

I needed to escape mentally. What many people didn't know about me was that I had a passion for writing and had a very active imagination. As I stood there inhaling his sauerkraut breath, I imagined that I was with someone else and that I was someplace else. I pictured that he was this boy named Aaron that I had the hugest crush on at my old school. I felt my lips connect with his and it didn't seem so bad.

That is until he shoved his large cow tongue down my throat. It was taking everything in me not to scream, "Fuck you and your deal!" But I knew that wouldn't help me at all. I would have to fully cooperate, if I planned on being reunited with my sister. Unfortunately, thoughts of Aaron were not enough to distract me from this grotesque piece of shit standing before me.

Wintress was my primary motivation for saying yes. I would just have to divert my focus on her and take this one for the team. His kisses were sloppy and hungry. It felt as if he was literally sucking my face off. He then began to lick aimlessly all over my face like a damn dog. I nearly gagged from the lingering stench of his breath on my face.

His breathing was heavy...almost animalistic as he forcefully pushed me onto the bed and started removing his clothes. I involuntarily frowned once he'd removed his shirt and I noticed that his fucking tits were bigger than mine. Thankfully he was so consumed it his own thoughts that it went unnoticed. He looked like a hairy ass bear.

Skin tags were scattered all over his rotund frame. But the worst was yet to come. I almost died when he pulled his slacks down and this bastard was wearing the dingiest pair of tighty whities known to balls and ass. The sight was just unbearable. I'm pretty sure I gagged internally.

"Take your clothes off baby. I've been yearning to see that lovely body of yours," he lustfully replied.

I stood up and did as I was told. I removed my cotton pajama set, leaving my bra and panties on.

"Take everything off!" he ordered impatiently.

I pulled my bra over my head and slowly slithered out of my red panties. I heard him gasp once I stood up and faced him booty butt ass naked. I didn't even bother trying to cover up. My inhibitions went out the window. I could never be embarrassed of anything on my body in front of this big bitch. Besides, I knew he would just tell me to move my hands anyway.

I was finally beginning to understand how this bullshit arrangement worked. Don swiftly rolled his big ass drawls down over his wide flat ass. Throughout this entire bullshit ordeal, I found comfort in one thing. That one thing was the fact that he was packing a baby dick. His dick was about the length of my thumb, but the girth was slightly thicker. This baby dicked fucker had the nerve to have these big humongous balls chilling beneath that little scrawny shit. Similar to his chest, his balls were hairy as hell.

To top it all off, Mrs. Douglas hadn't bothered to circumcise his repulsive ass. It was all I could do to prevent myself from shuddering in disgust. I internally cried knowing that I'd be sharing something so intimately sacred with Don. He came over and begin to rub on my dry pussy.

"You have sandpaper pussy over here baby. I'm going to have to take care of that and then you will take care of me," he whispered.

With that he dove headfirst into my pussy. The sensation was different. I tried not to like it because I did not like the person doing it. He truly did have one of the longest and thickest tongues I had ever seen. I covered my face with a pillow in the hopes that I could once again imagine that he was Aaron. Once I replaced Don's head with Aaron's head, I found myself moaning loudly and grabbing at his hair...or lack thereof.

I was gyrating my pussy against his tongue. Don's long tongue was swiftly beating on my clit. I felt him exploring my folds while pinching my right nipple. This pushed me over the edge, and I felt myself begin to shake uncontrollably while fluid gushed out of my sweet spot.

"Unhhhh that's right! That feels soooo good Aaron!!!" I whimpered riding on my orgasmic waves.

"Are you fucking kidding me Autumn?! What the fuck did I just tell your ass? Hunh?! I don't even want you giving my pussy away in your fantasies. Like it or not you are just going to have to get use to *me*. I will give you a pass because this is all new to you, but don't let that fucking shit happen again. Oh, and don't think that I didn't notice how you frowned up in disgust once I removed my shirt. Your ass better get it together!" He snapped.

"Now it is my turn," he replied as he motioned to his miniature dick.

"Don, can we skip this part? I've never done it before and I never really wanted to either...unless maybe for my husband one day," I pleaded.

SLAP!!!

"Maybe I have not made myself clear. You can't even hypothetically be with another man. What the fuck do you mean skip this part?! You didn't ask me to skip eating your little dry ass pussy, did you? Autumn, suck my fucking cock now!!!" He growled through clenched yellowed teeth.

His dumpy ass was turning red and shit.

I threw my hands up in surrender, "Okay okay, take it easy Don. I'm sorry. I just don't know what I'm supposed to do. I'm nervous, that's all."

He shook his big balding head at me.

"For someone who is so smart, you sure are playing awfully stupid right now. I like getting my cock sucked, so you may as well get used to it. Just suck on it like a Popsicle and you better not bite my shit!" He warned while stroking his enlarged clitoris. Yes, enlarged clitoris...not dick!

As he was stroking his dick back and forth, I noticed a thick coat of smegma each time his foreskin was retracted. I wasn't sure if it were normal or not. As my mouth inched closer to his lap, I noticed that his dick had a cheesy odor while his scrotum smelled a bit musty. All of his different aromas sent a wave of nausea over me.

As I was about to ask him about the smegma and the possibility of him showering first, he roughly jammed his dick inside of my mouth. Internally I was screaming at the top of my lungs, but externally I played it cool. He guided my head up and down on his dick.

I was able to easily fit his entire length into my mouth. I did my best to tune out his animal growls mixed with his feminine moans. He grabbed onto the back of my head and pounded away into my mouth as if he were fucking a pussy. All the while I was extra careful not to bite or graze his dick with my teeth.

Finally, he pulled his dick out of my mouth and ordered me to lie down.

"You're a fast learner Autumn. You were absolutely great,

but now I'm ready to burst that sweet little cherry of yours. Open up," he ordered.

I dreadfully opened my legs and cringed as he bent down to give my pussy a quick slobbery lick for lubrication.

As he stroked himself and was about to enter me, I interrupted him by asking, "Don can you please use a condom? I'm not on any birth control."

He ignored me and began rubbing his dick head along my slit. I felt him slap my clit a couple of times with it as well. I then felt his eager dick sitting just outside of my opening.

"You're going to probably want to kiss me right now," he stated matter of factly.

I glared at him and highly doubted that I would ever *want* to kiss his ass under any circumstance. I assumed I didn't have much of a choice as I accepted his tongue. As he deeply kissed me, he held both of my arms above my head. That's when I felt him begin to push my pussy walls aside to accommodate his dick. I sharply drew in a breath and attempted to tell him to get the fuck off of me. He had my hands locked in place and was muffling my cries with his lips.

The pain was excruciating as he continued to work himself inside of me. I cried so hard that I felt snot streaming out of my nose. Even if my hands were free, I wouldn't have bothered to wipe it. He continued to force me to moan into his mouth as he kissed me. Who knew that something so small could inflict so much pain? Tears were soaking my pillow as I felt him stroke in and out of me.

He was pounding me mercilessly with no regard to this being my first time. At least he did free my hands by this time and had stopped kissing me. He was too engulfed in his own ecstasy to realize that I felt as if I were being split into two. He was going wild and I couldn't wait for it to be over.

He was sweating profusely, and I was becoming more and more irate with each bead of sweat that dripped onto my body. The fat fuck had the nerve to ask me whose pussy it was. I ignored his funky ass. I know many people say that sex eventually begins to feel better after a few minutes, but that pleasure never came.

The longer he pounded my pussy, the drier I became. The drier I became the more painful his strokes were. I could've done a naked cartwheel when I watched his no neck having ass thrust inside of me one last time before releasing his unwanted seeds inside of my violated pussy.

I felt so disgustingly sticky. I was covered in his putrid sweat, saliva and now I felt his semen slowly seeping out of my gaping pussy and was running towards my asshole. I wanted to make a bee line into the shower, but he wanted to cuddle.

"Autumn, I'm so happy this happened between us, I want you to know that I will always be here for you. You are mine now. I'm sorry for being so rough with you, but I just wanted you to get use to me. It won't always be this bad. In fact, you will grow to love having sex. God knows I have thoroughly enjoyed what we just shared.

In regard to me wearing a condom...I will never wear one with you. The sooner you accept that fact, the better. I loved cumming inside of you. If you happen to get pregnant, we will deal with it at that time. It wouldn't be the end of the world," he declared while breathing heavily with his out of shape ass.

I listened to him wondering what in the hell I had gotten myself in to!!!

SHEENA PERRY

« Chapter 18 Indecisive »

The Past "Alicia"

I KNOW MANY OF YOU are heartbroken over my abortion. The truth is...I couldn't go through with it. I had convinced myself that it had to be done in order to rid myself of that piece of shit, Mike. I thought by ending my pregnancy I could dump him and never have to look at him ever again. In the short time that I have been pregnant, I had already become attached to my little peanut.

On the day that Cee Cee accompanied me to the clinic, I was ready. I couldn't wait to have the entire ordeal behind me. However, after listening to how the procedure was done and speaking to the grief counselors, I knew in my heart that I wanted to keep my baby. I expressed my apprehensions to the nurse and doctor. They were very nice and supportive. Of course, they were unable to refund the money, but I didn't care.

I told them that I wanted to rest for a bit and gather my thoughts before going back into the waiting area. The nurse told me that it was a slow day, so they were able to accommodate my request. Besides, they had practically been paid for nothing. In the meantime, the doctor wrote a prescription for prenatal vitamins and Cipro since my urinalysis came back showing that I had a mild urinary tract infection.

I of course led Cee Cee to believe that the medication was related to me having the abortion. I don't know why I just didn't tell her that I had changed my mind, but I just couldn't. I limped out into the waiting area to make it appear that I was in pain. I cried all the way home and into the evening. The tears were very real. I was not crying over an abortion as Cee Cee thought, but I cried because I was conflicted. I cried for all the things that I'd potentially have to give up as a single parent.

I didn't know what to do. I truly believed that Mike would have hurt me, had I gotten rid of his baby. I no longer wanted to be with him so I wept because I knew that I would have to raise my baby alone. Great hardships lay ahead. I didn't want this for myself. This was not in my plans. My baby deserved a lot more than what I'd be able to offer them.

It was too late to cry over spilled milk now. Life had to go on. I just had to find a way to break the news to my mother. I had decided that I would tell both my mom and Cee Cee together, but only when I absolutely had to. I didn't know how to form the words. How could I blurt out that I was expecting to my mother?

Mike was the only person aware that I was still pregnant. He never knew of my plans to terminate my pregnancy. He continued to call me nonstop. He had delivered flowers and showed up unannounced numerous times. I had been lucky and had managed to dodge him at school. I always showed up a little late and left a little early. I was ready to move on.

I was not looking to date seeing how I was pregnant and had recently gotten out of a relationship. I know some women may feel that I should just forgive Mike. Give him a second chance. They would convince me that it was a one-time fling...a momentary slip-up. But I am a firm believer that once a cheater, always a cheater. I was tempted by the opposite sex just as much, if not more than Mike was. Did I cheat on him? Hell no! I never even entertained the thought.

It was the ultimate sign of disrespect. As if that wasn't bad enough, he threatened me and put his hands on me. My mom had instilled in me my self-worth and I knew that I deserved better than that shit.

My father was a no-good cheater. He played my mother bigtime. He had her thinking that she was his one and only, yet he had an entire family back at home. I don't think she ever got over that betrayal. What they did was inexcusable. There was no coming back from that shit. Fuck Mike! Fuck my father! Fuck men!

One day while getting my English Literature book out of my locker, I felt a pair of arms wrap around my waist cradling my lower abdomen. I immediately tensed up because only one person would be bold enough to touch me this way. I roughly snatched away from him and shot him an evil glare. I then resumed grabbing my belongings from my locker.

"Alicia, we really need to talk. You've ignored me long enough. I've apologized a million and one times. I've given you more than enough time and space. It is now time for us to get back on track. We need to be mature about this girl. We have a fucking baby on the way. I've missed you so much, baby. Please stop being mad at me. A nigga's sorry baby! Have you missed daddy?"

I ignored him as I closed my locker and started walking in the direction of my next class. I had nothing to say to his sorry ass. I didn't feel the need to waste my breath or energy. I had already told him it was over.

"Alicia, are you freaking serious right now? Do you not hear me talking to you?! Enough is enough. You are pregnant with my seed, yet you have been dodging me like your stupid ass doesn't hear me talking to you. I will be by later so that we can talk. Don't answer the door and see what happens. I'm not playing with your childish ass anymore!" Mike yelled at the top of his lungs to my back.

I continued to walk down the hall with my head held high although I was extremely embarrassed about him exposing my pregnancy to half of the school...including Cee Cee. Her face held a puzzled look as she stared at me from her locker. I tuned everyone out and ignored Mike's threat. The remainder of the school day was uneventful. I had been avoiding Cee Cee, but I was her ride home, so it was time to face the music. We were both quiet once she made it to my mother's car. After a few minutes, I could feel her gaze burning a hole through the right side of my face.

"Just ask me already Cee Cee, damn!"

"Is it true?" She questioned.

I started to play stupid, but thought better of it. I decided to finally come clean. I hated lying to my bestie.

"Yes, I am still pregnant. I don't know why I lied. I guess I didn't want you to look at me differently for deciding to keep the baby. I am so sorry for lying to you!" I stated as I began to cry.

"Alicia, you are family to me. I will never ever judge you. I have no room to judge. You know that I will support you no matter what you decide to do. Honestly, I'm happy that you've decided to keep the baby. I'm going to be an auntie! I hope it's a boy. Everyone seems to be having girls lately! Now heifer, cheer up! I be that baby's pappi!" She exclaimed with a Colgate smile.

She instantly made me feel as if everything was going to be alright. I couldn't help, but to burst out into a fit of laughter in her presence.

"Cee Cee, I still have to tell my mom. I don't know how she is going to handle this news. I think she'll support me regardless, I just feel like such a failure. I'm another statistic, you know? She keeps asking me what's going on between Mike and me.

She has noticed that I've been ignoring his dog ass. I really don't want to, but I guess I have to bite the bullet and get it over with. Although I no longer want to be with him, I'd never stop him from being there for our baby. I'd never be that type of woman," I admitted.

She asked, "How do you think he is going to handle you not wanting to be with him? Do you want me to be there when he comes over later?"

"Girl no, I'll be fine. He is just gonna have to deal with it. My mom should be there anyway. We have to learn how to co-parent without beefing all the time," I shrugged nonchalantly.

"Just be careful friend. I never did trust his black ass. Call me and let me know how everything goes," she stated as we pulled up to her house.

"I always do boo," I teased.

We hugged before parting ways.

« Chapter 19 The Trap »

The Past "Mike"

I PULLED UP TO MY lady's crib dressed to kill. I had gotten my hair cut earlier and I smelled like a million bucks. I came bearing gifts, of course. I bought Alicia flowers, a teddy bear and an "I'm sorry" card. I was trying to do everything that I could to redeem myself. I knew that she was still upset with me, but it was time for her to let bygones be bygones. I'm only human. I'm a flawed man.

Men sometimes cheat from time to time. It didn't mean that I loved her any less. I just needed something different sometimes. Especially since Alicia didn't like trying out new things. I was willing to overlook her shortcomings, but she needed to do the same. She wasn't perfect either, but I loved her regardless.

What females failed to realize is, when we fuck around with other women, they are only getting the dick. Nothing else. There were no feelings involved. Hell, they should thank the side bitches for taking some of their responsibilities away. I'm a nasty bastard. As such, I require nasty things in the bedroom.

How can you deny me certain acts, then become upset when I find another bitch who is more than willing to perform them? Bitches can be so selfish at times. I don't think that I could ever be completely faithful, but I have been cutting back a lot. I put myself on coochie restrictions.

I've cut off pretty much all these broads except for my ex and occasionally Sha'keisha. I still had a lot of love for Tamar. After all she was my first love. She was a brown skin beauty who reminded me of the actress, Malinda Williams. She was not thick like Alicia. Instead she was petite and curvy. The reason why she would never be my number one lady again is because she was a gold digger. She fucked with me because of my earning potential.

She was older than me and had my head in the clouds back in the day. I've flipped the switch on her ass though. Although I was no longer in love with her, I still had love for her. I just couldn't seem to shake her. It turns out that I had gotten her ass pregnant again. She wasn't trying to have an abortion this time, no matter how much I begged. I had fucked up royally.

Alicia and Tamar were the only two women that I ever entered raw. I know I should have been strapping up, but those were my bitches. I knew no other niggas had touched either one of them. Alicia was dominating every department over Tamar with the exception of matters pertaining to the bedroom.

Tamar was down for whatever sexually. But she was also very entitled and didn't like to work. She'd graduated two years ago, yet didn't feel the need to make any moves beyond that point. She was one of those women who were content with living off the system her entire life.

She wasn't much of a cook or a housekeeper either. I guess you could call me an enabler. I made my money through boosting. This shit was temporary though. I was hustling just until I was drafted. I knew early on that I'd never be a dope boy. I always copped the dopest shit and made a killing off the people from around the way. I took care of Tamar financially and was getting fed up with it. Her lack of motivation and drive was turning me off.

I was not thrilled about having a baby on the way with Tamar, but I couldn't be mad either. Neither of us had done anything to prevent this pregnancy. I knew she had trapped me in hopes of a bigger pay day once I made it to the pros. Her shady ass was so transparent.

Alicia on the other hand, now, I got that ass pregnant on purpose. She warned me from day one that she'd never forgive me for cheating. Apparently, her pops was a hoe and she didn't want to deal with that shit in her own relationship...blah blah blah. I whole-heartedly believed her when she said that she'd *try* to leave me. And I honestly did try to be faithful, but it proved to be a difficult feat. Possibly even impossible.

I knew that one day my fucked-up ways were going to come and bite me in the ass. Especially after finding out that Tamar was pregnant. Tamar knew about Alicia, however, Alicia had no idea who Tamar was. Tamar was over six months pregnant now, so I knew that I had to work fast on securing a future with Alicia. Some call it trapping...but I didn't really give a damn.

I made sure to keep track of Alicia's periods as well as ovulation window. I made sure we had sex at least two times a day while she was ovulating. Initially after popping her cherry, I'd start off wearing a rubber so she wouldn't trip. Then I would slide it off after a few strokes. I was the only guy that she'd ever slept with, so she was oblivious to it at first. Then she started to learn the difference between my cum and her own.

By that time, we had done away with condoms. I'd just assure her that I would pull out, yet I always conveniently forgot. I knew neither of us was ready for a baby, however, I had to ensure that we shared some type of eternal bond. She would never be able to get too far away from me with my child. I would never allow her to leave me anyway. She belonged to me. She's my bitch.

∞

I quickly snapped out of my thoughts before I rang her doorbell. I performed a quick breath check. I was glad that her mother's primary car was not in the driveway yet. We needed our privacy. I wasn't sure if her mom even knew about this pregnancy. Moments later my baby answered the door looking beautiful ass ever.

She was glowing. She wore no makeup on her flawless skin and her hair was pulled up into a messy bun on top of her head. She was still the most beautiful woman in the world to me. My seed had made her even more beautiful...if that was even possible. She was wearing a simple summer dress and her favorite pink slippers.

"Are you going to invite me in?" I asked after she coldly glared at me without saying anything.

Instead of replying, she stepped back so that I could enter her house. I handed her the flowers, bear and the card. After she closed the door, I leaned down in an attempt to give her a hug and a kiss. She quickly jumped back in order to avoid my embrace. I must admit, this hurt my feelings a lot. It pissed me off too.

She had never acted this way towards me before. I kept my cool as I followed her into the living room. She tossed all the gifts that I had brought, carelessly onto the table. She then sat on the opposite end of the couch. She had her arms folded under her breasts.

She turned to me and finally uttered the first words I'd heard her speak since entering her house, "You said that you wanted to talk, so talk. I don't have all night either!"

I know I had fucked up, but this bitch was trying my patience.

"Bitch who the fuck do you think you are talking to? I've been trying to make up for what happened. I'm sick of kissing your ungrateful ass. What do I need to do or say to make you aware of the fact that I am truly sorry? A nigga is sorry baby. I didn't fuck that ugly ass hoe. Do you forgive me? I miss talking to you. I miss seeing you every day. I miss you cheering for me. I miss making love to you. Can we just move past this shit?!"

She paused as if in deep thought. I was hopeful before she replied, "Mike, I loved you with all of my heart. We must maintain a cordial friendship for the sake of our baby...but there is no more us. We are finished. Cheating is a hang up for me. I pray that we can remain friends. I'd never keep you from our baby. You are welcome to attend all the appointments as well as the birth. I wouldn't deny you those experiences."

I tilted my head to the side as I looked at her because she must've bumped her head if she thought that I was about to sit on the sidelines while she messed with another nigga and had him raising my baby.

"Come on Alicia baby. There is no need to take it to this extreme. You've made your point. We can work through this one little problem. Baby we've never even had a fight before this. Are you seriously going to allow another bitch that I didn't even smash come in between us? This shit will never happen again," I lied.

"Mike, it's over. You wanted to talk, and we have. I think that you sho...."

Before I realized what I was doing, I had slapped fire to her face. I then grabbed her bun and dragged her ass into her bedroom. She was screaming bloody murder which only infuriated me even more. Why the fuck was she acting afraid of me?! I slung her onto her bed by her hair and covered her mouth and nose with my large hand. I told her that I was not going to remove my hand until she chilled the fuck out.

After she stopped fighting me, I whispered, "Bitch, you will never leave me. I will kill your ass before that happens. If I can't have you, you better believe the next nigga never will either. We are going to be a family. I'm going to marry you one day.

I'm sorry for getting a little rough with you, but you've been disrespecting me a lot lately. You have to stop making me so mad. I don't like being this way with you. Okay baby? I love you. Please forgive me already," I said with tears streaming down my face.

I felt terrible for putting my hands on her, but she didn't seem to respond to words well.

"Come here baby." I coaxed.

For the first time today, she complied. I slowly began to kiss her face, paying special attention to the hand print I'd left on her right cheek. I was surprised when she didn't resist me. I kissed her soft sweet lips and after a few moments, she slowly started kissing me back. I had missed her dearly in the short time that she had been avoiding me. She was smelling so good and felt even better in my arms.

My kisses trailed down to her neck. I knew that her hotspot had always been the nape of her neck. I skillfully twirled my tongue in various directions followed by me blowing lightly on her skin. I noticed her rock-hard nipples standing at full attention beneath the thin material of her dress.

Alicia could say that she didn't want to be with me until she was blue in the face; however, the body never lies. I knew her body better than she did. Lifting her dress up, I decided to give her perky mounds the attention they so desperately needed.

She didn't have the biggest pair of tits, but they were more than a mouthful. I could devour her breasts all day. She whimpered softly as I feasted on her fleshy mountains. I licked and slurped as she arched her back and massaged my head. Alicia was soon moaning and asking for more. I slid her panties to the side and just stared in awe at her plump wet mound. It felt like a century had gone by since I had seen her pretty pink pussy. My pussy.

Her slit was glistening with sweet nectar. I couldn't wait to taste her. I also made sure she drank lots of water and ate pineapples. I don't care what anyone says, that shit worked! I begin to kiss and lick on her inner thighs. I knew it would drive her up a wall. I begin to tweak her right nipple as I watched her lick on her left one. That shit almost made me bust on sight.

I didn't even know she could do that. Her long tongue flicked over her large erect nipples just as I popped her clit into my mouth. She gasped and threw her head back. I nibbled and hummed on her pearl driving her wild. I then slithered my tongue up and down her slit before plunging my tongue into her warm, sweet hole.

She was so wet that my entire face was covered in her dew. I loved getting my face messy. She was screaming loudly and sexily humping my face. She was begging me to fuck her. I stood up and swiftly removed my clothes before she could back pedal. I climbed on top of her and kissed her tenderly.

I loved when she tasted herself. I then spread her legs apart. It would've been nice to have gotten some head first, but Alicia wasn't down with that. I was so horny that I noticed my dick oozing precum onto the bed. I must have really been missing her because I noticed that happening a lot lately. I slid my throbbing member up and down Alicia's moist slit, ready to plunge deep inside of my baby.

She then said, "Mike, do you have protection? I know that I'm already pregnant, but for other things...you know?"

"Yeah baby I got you," I said as I swiftly buried myself to the hilt into Alicia.

I knew she was in pain by the way she scratched the hell out of my back and screamed out. I did that intentionally. She was going to learn to stop asking me that dumb shit. Whoever said that pregnant pussy was the best, was on the ball with that shit. Her shit felt so different, but in a good way. That pussy was extra gushy. She always felt amazing, but she was now wetter, tighter and warmer.

I could literally hear and feel her love juice splashing onto my balls and running down my thighs. That noise was intoxicating. Her cries of passion made me work harder to please her. Her moans beckoned me to stroke her faster and deeper. I was striving to reach places that I hadn't in our previous encounters. I was trying to fuck her into submission.

"Are you still trying to leave me baby?" I asked as I turned her over onto her stomach.

Without waiting for a response, I slapped her on her fat

ass. I then plunged back into her warmth before she could even compose herself.

"You're trying to leave me, hunh? Your ass isn't going anywhere...are you? No one else is about to get any of this good pussy. This shit belongs to me. I'm your first and your last. You forgive me baby?" I continued talking to her as I deep stroked her ass from the back.

I pushed down on her back to deepen the arch. I watched my ten-inch third leg slide in and out of her moist hole. My shit was glistening and wet as it played peekaboo with her warm tunnel. Since she was playing mute, I decided to show her ass no mercy. I drilled into her ass like a jack hammer until she screamed out for me to slow down.

"I'll slow down when you answer my question. Are we back together?" I bellowed as our skin slapped together. "Are we?!"

"Yes, Mike! Yes, we are back together baby," she cried out.

"Do you forgive me?"

"Yes!"

"Are you ever going to give my pussy away?"

"No, never baby!"

"Do you love me?"

"Of course!"

"I love you too, girl," I growled before sending off one of the biggest nuts of my life to her cervix. If she wasn't already knocked up, she would've been after this shit.

"Where is your mom baby?" I inquired, attempting to catch my breath.

"She called me before you came. She volunteered to stay over and help at the hospital." Alicia replied breathlessly.

That was all I needed to hear before laying behind her and placing my semi-erect penis back into her dank hole. I loved her pussy so much that I always slept with my dick inside of her. Our sweaty bodies became one as we continued to breathe heavily.

I closed my eyes with the first real smile that I had in weeks. I knew then that I could never let Alicia find out about Tamar and our baby. My smile was quickly replaced with worry as sleep evaded me.

« Chapter 20 These Hoes Ain't Loyal »

The Past "Eli"

I HAD BEEN SITTING in front of this building for the last three hours. I had been casing this place out for a couple of weeks now. As usual, there was not a lot going on tonight. I had checked on my trap houses prior to coming here. I was getting hungry and could use a nightcap from one of the dime pieces I messed with from time to time.

Don't get me wrong, I was starting to care about Celeste, but I had needs. Needs that she was not yet ready to fulfill. I'd have blue balls messing with her little ass. I could've fucked her when I had her at my house. My conscience got the better part of me. I shocked myself when I made the decision not to have sex with her in order to win the bet.

Initially when she suggested that we turn the lights off I was a little annoyed. I worried that my camcorder wouldn't be able to show us having sex. Then I concluded that any idiot would still be able to listen to the recording and know that the sex was real. However, bragging rights and a thousand dollars didn't seem worth dragging her name through the mud. She deserved better than that.

I'd be lying if I said I didn't want to fuck the shit out of her. She tasted so good and her coochie gripped the hell out of my fingers. I did need to talk to her about shaving though. She had the 1970's fro going on downtown. I didn't want to embarrass her last time by mentioning it. But she needed to know because I didn't care for hairy pussy.

As I waited in the car, I decided to snort a couple of lines in the hopes that it would give me a little bit of energy. I had been balancing hustling, school, sports and my bitches. My main bitch was Kennedy. While she had the potential to be wifey material, I was simply not trying to cuff her ass. She had scandalous ways about her.

She was well known for setting people up. While she had been beneficial to me several times, I knew it was only a matter of time before I ended up on the losing team. No matter how much I made it clear that she would never obtain a title from me, she would somehow convince herself that she was more than she was. Her pussy was cool, but her head was A1.

She was sexy as fuck, but her ways made her very unattractive. I definitely had to keep the fact that I had smashed Kennedy's little twat into extinction from Celeste. I knew they didn't get along and I wanted Celeste.

I don't know why, but there was something about her that made me want to explore the possibilities. As I said before, she was cut from a different cloth. She could care less if I had ten dollars or ten million. I knew Kennedy on the other hand wouldn't give my ass a second glance if I wasn't out here making big moves.

Snapping out of my thoughts, I refocused my attention on the task at hand. Although my targets worked here, they were rarely present. Every time I did catch a momentary glance of them, I grew angry and instantly wanted to attack. However, I had to plan this out correctly. I'd have to be patient. I wanted them both to suffer.

As I fantasized about all of the different ways that I could bring them anguish, an idea popped into my head. I'd destroy them both, but first, I was going to ensure that everything around them collapsed before I made my big attack. Deciding to call it a night, I pulled off satiated by the plans that I had in store for their sick asses.

∞

The next day, I decided to go and pay Celeste a visit at her job before she got off. It was always hard to get in touch with her once she made it home. Pulling in front of the mall, I checked myself out in the mirror. I didn't want her to catch me with coke on my face again. I was slipping. Maybe it was time for me to cut back a little bit.

I was happy that she was as naïve and innocent as she was. Not many people would have fallen for my "powder" story. I'm not sure how she would react to me occasionally snorting lines. But what I did know was, I didn't want to find out.

Satisfied with my appearance, I exited my car. As I walked into the clothing store, I noticed several thirsty women sending me lustful looks. I was used to it and pretended not to notice. I wasn't thinking about them. The only thing any of those broads were capable of doing for me was getting my dick wet. I was looking for more than that shit.

As I made it to the back of the store, I spotted Cee Cee. She was always so beautiful to me. Naturally beautiful. Once she spotted me, she smiled brightly.

"Hey baby, what are you doing here?" She inquired after hugging me.

"I kind of missed you and wanted to take you somewhere. Ask your supervisor if you can leave early today."

"You only kind of missed me?" She questioned poking her bottom lip out.

"You know that I missed the hell out of you baby girl!" I said kissing her soft full lips.

"Well it is pretty slow right now, let me check with Joe to see if I can leave. Where are you taking me anyway?"

"It's a surprise with your little nosey ass. You'll see when we get there. Just trust me girl, you're going to like it. Do you trust me?" I asked.

She smiled, licked her lips and replied, "It all depends boo. Let's just put it this way, I trust you enough."

She then turned in the direction of her supervisor's office. I couldn't help myself as I smacked her on her round ass. I watched as the slap caused a ripple effect to occur in her ass. I instantly felt blood rush to my dick. I knew I was going to have to pay Kennedy's nagging ass a visit once I left Cee Cee for the day.

Cee Cee was in the back for nearly ten minutes before she resurfaced. She seemed different. She was bothered by something, however, she continued to reiterate that she was fine.

I figured her supervisor had probably given her a hard time about leaving early. She told me that he hadn't and to just drop it. I decided not to ruin our date together and to revisit the conversation later.

Once leaving her job, I decided to lighten the mood by tickling her and kissing her all over her face. Soon, she was back in good spirits. I got a bad vibe from her punk ass boss. If he had said something out of the way to my girl, I was going to have to deal with his ass too. Something about him was off. However, he'd met his match.

I first took Cee Cee to north city to a place called Crown Candy. They had some of the best ice cream in the Lou. We people watched and talked about our plans for the future. She was so smart and as tough as nails. She'd been through a lot, but didn't allow her circumstances to throw a wrench into her future plans. Once we left Crown Candy, I took her to my uncle's car dealership. He sold a variety of cars, but was a huge fan of foreign cars. Cee Cee looked confused as I pulled onto the lot and got out.

As I opened her door and assisted her out of the car she asked, "Eli, what are we doing here? Are you thinking about getting a new car? I love the car that you have already."

I nodded my head and said, "I am getting a car today, but not for me...for you baby. I don't like you having to rely on me or anyone else to get around. You've been working hard and if I can alleviate at least one of your stressors, then I will. You're worth it. My uncle owns this dealership, so look around and find something that you like. He will give us a good deal.

After looking around for thirty minutes, I noticed that Cee Cee kept scoping out a red 1996 BMW 328I Convertible.

Although it wasn't my personal favorite, I replied, "It looks like you've made your decision. Do you want to take this car on a test drive?"

Her eyes lit up and she quickly nodded her head. I found my uncle and he allowed me to take her on a test drive alone. Cee Cee excitedly tampered around in the car for a while prior to driving off. It was great seeing her smile so brightly. I wish that I could always keep those smiles on her beautiful face. The car suited her.

My uncle of course made me a great deal. As Cee Cee filled out the necessary paperwork, she turned to me and said, "Thank you so much for doing this for me Eli. No one has ever done anything like this for me. You will never know how much this all means to me. You're the best boyfriend in the world! I love my new car. Is this the special gift that you had promised me?"

"It's part of it, but you have to wait for the rest of it gorgeous. You're very welcome by the way. I was happy to do this for you. Remember that I will always have your back," I stated seriously looking into her eyes.

She smiled with tears in her eyes before giving me a hug.

"Well look baby, I have some errands to run. Let's meet up tomorrow after school, okay? Now you can pick me up for dates. I'm not giving your ass any gas money either," I joked.

She softly punched me in the arm as she laughed.

"Okay love, I cannot wait to show Alicia my brand-new car!!! I'll see you tomorrow handsome."

She gave me a final tight hug and a long passionate kiss. I watched her get into her car and pull off. I glanced down at my pager and noticed that Kennedy had been blowing me up. Blowing a frustrated raspberry, I decided to just head over to her crib instead of calling. Her mother never gave a damn if I came over and fucked her daughter in the next room.

After making the short drive to Kennedy's housing projects, I noticed the same people out on the block. I knew everyone had to be tired of the same redundancy known as their lives. Hell, I was exhausted for them. How could everyone be so content with so little? They were content with the occasional meager handouts. I knew I was no angel and had little room to judge, however, every move that I made was to secure my future.

Once I pulled up in front of Kennedy's apartment, she was

sitting on the porch gossiping with her friend who also happened to be her next-door neighbor, Gia. That shit turned me off. I hated bitches with no direction. She better be glad that her head game was strong, otherwise I would've just pulled off.

Approaching the pathetic pair, I greeted them both with a simple, "What's up?" I didn't even look in Gia's direction. Truthfully, she was extremely attractive and resembled Chilli from the R&B group TLC. She was pretty and felt the need to make everyone else aware of it every chance she got. That made her ugly as hell to me. Plus, she was disloyal.

Here she was smiling in Kennedy's face today, yet two days ago my dick was plunged deep into her asshole. That was the only perk to dealing with her. She was unafraid to take the pipe in the backdoor. Most girls our age wasn't down for that. She knew that Kennedy was in love with me, yet she still fucked with me. They were supposed to be friends.

"Dang Eli, what type of greeting is that?" Gia quipped.

Ignoring her obsolete ass, I turned to Kennedy, "Aye, you've been blowing my pager up all day. I'm here now, so are you going to use that mouth to continue yapping to bird brain over there, or are you ready to swallow this nut?"

Both of them looked embarrassed because I had put them on blast. Unfortunately for them both, I gave zero fucks about their feelings. If either of them decided not to mess with me anymore, I wouldn't shed a single tear or give them a first thought...let alone a second one. While they both stood there with stupid expressions on their faces, I walked past them and entered Kennedy's small, but tidy apartment.

Before entering her room, I heard Kennedy say, "Girl, let

me get on in there and see what has my man tripping. I'm sorry he said those things about you. He didn't mean that shit."

"Like hell I didn't," I mumbled closing the bedroom door preparing to remove my clothes.

Kennedy came in moments later asking if I were okay. I told her that I was cool. She then asked why I treated her the way that I did.

"You know I love you Eli. I have always loved you. Why can't you see that? I've always been your ride or die, yet you treat me like a hoe. Why don't you love me?"

"Look Ken, I do have love for you, but as I have told you a thousand times before, I don't want to be with you. I'm not trying to hurt your feelings, but we will never be together. You are a pretty girl and will make some guy happy one day, I'm just not that guy. Besides, my interest lies elsewhere."

"What the hell do you mean your interest lies elsewhere?! Who are you fucking around with? What does she have that I don't Eli?" She tearfully snapped.

"All of that is irrelevant right now. Stop lying to people and telling them that I am your man. That shit isn't cool shorty. You're making an uncomplicated situation very complicated. You knew what time it was when we started fucking around. I told you that I wasn't looking for anything serious with you. My feelings haven't changed. With that being said, are you ready to do what I came over here for?" I honestly stated.

"Also, Gia is not your friend. I don't know why you hang out with her conceited ass."

"Fuck you Eli! You think that you can keep treating me like this? I'm not going to wait around for forever. Go have your new little girlfriend suck your dick. I'm not sucking shit! As a matter of fact, you can leave. Get the fuck out!"

I instantly snapped and wanted to knock her ass the fuck out. Not because she was asking me to leave, but I didn't appreciate her disrespecting my girl.

I snatched her up, "Bitch, you better watch your tone and your tongue when you talk to me. Never disrespect my girl again. I will leave. I've never been pressed and begged a hoe for sex. Don't page me anymore either. I'm out!"

I pushed her away from me causing her to stumble backwards. Catching her balance, she immediately went into panic mode.

"Baby please don't leave. I'm sorry. I didn't mean that shit. I'm just hurt and don't understand why we can't be together. Calm down, okay? Laydown and let me take care of you," she suggested unfastening my jeans.

I smiled inwardly because this was the same song and dance that I played with Kennedy. She knew she wasn't going anywhere. However, this shit was growing old. Dealing with all this drama was no longer worth being able to coat her tonsils with my seeds. Kennedy dropped to her knees in front of me.

She never gave me any of that lazy, belly laying head. She got on her knees like the good bitch that she was. I was considerate and handed her a pillow from her bed to cushion her knees against the hard floor. I watched as she licked on the underside of my throbbing member. She placed soft kisses on the tip of my dick before swirling her moist tongue around it as well.

She gave sloppy, noisy head. She slurped loudly as her warm mouth swallowed my entire dick. I watched as her small hands both wrapped around my shaft skillfully stroking me while her head bobbed up and down. The feeling of being halfway down her throat was unreal.

She spit on my dick several times only to slurp it back up. She then gave my balls the attention they needed. She licked, sucked and then hummed on them before slipping a moist finger into my asshole. That shit almost sent me over the edge as I nearly came down her throat.

I pulled my dick out of her mouth for a moment to regain control. Pulling her up into a standing position, I quickly slid on a condom. I then picked her up and lowered her onto my erect pipe. As I stood there, she began to bounce up and down. I felt a trail of her juices sliding down onto my balls. Her wetness turned me on so much that I couldn't help but to begin stroking upwards to match her thrust.

I slapped her on the ass periodically assuring her that she was doing a great job. After my arms grew tired of holding her up, I gently lowered her to her feet. I then laid on the bed and told her to ride me in the reverse cowgirl position.

She happily obliged. Watching her lower her fat pussy onto my dick should have been a work of art. While her pussy was okay at best, she did have one of those twats that gripped your dick. I sat back and enjoyed watching my dick play peekaboo with her pussy.

I also enjoyed watching her asshole wink at me. As she rode me, I slipped a finger into her alluring brown eye. She immediately tensed up. She never allowed me to touch her asshole, but I knew she was letting me do it in order to prove a point. She wanted to compete with my girl, assuming that she allowed me to play with her ass too.

Soon she relaxed and I noticed that she was moaning even

more than usual. She was loving the ass play as much as I had. A lot of people are so closed-minded and viewed ass play as something that only gay men did. However, the definition of being gay is defined as being attracted to the same sex.

Nowhere in that definition does it state that having your ass played with by the *opposite* sex is gay. I wasn't attracted to men and would never allow one to touch me. A lot of men were missing out due to this unfounded stigma surrounding ass play. Then again, there were many men that enjoyed the shit, but would never admit it.

Feeling my nut rising to the surface, I began to rapidly thrust into Kennedy. I was beating her pussy up so roughly that I knew I was rearranging her organs. She was loudly moaning my name and crying out to the Lord. My breathing quickened as I swiftly removed myself from her. Although my dick was clad in a condom, I still refused to nut inside of these broads.

After emptying my seeds into the condom, I went to flush the condom and wash my dick off. Coming back into Kennedy's room, I noticed that her ass was out like a light. I was always able to put that ass to sleep.

Quietly redressing, I exited Kennedy's room. Passing through the living room, I noticed her mother laying on the couch in her robe. She had her legs cocked open and was furiously rubbing on her pearl. I shook my head at this old hoe. Her mom was still sexy as fuck, but damn she had no boundaries. I guess hearing me beat her daughter's walls down had that ancient kitty purring.

I walked over to the couch and replaced her hand with mine. I slid three fingers inside of Kennedy's mom while my other hand stroked her pearl. She was soon bucking wildly and creaming all over my hand. Removing my hand, I sniffed my fingers before sliding them into her mouth. I made her suck her juices off all the fingers I had just removed from her grey ass pussy.

Before turning to leave, I lowly whispered, "You're welcome Ms. Wet Pussy."

I made a mental note to see what that pussy was capable of at a later date. I was too tired today. Besides, I respected Kennedy enough to knock her mother's back out when she wasn't home. As soon as I made it to the porch, I ran straight into Gia's self-centered ass.

"I saw what you did. I was wondering how long you were going to pretend to enjoy playing in her wack ass pussy. Bring your yellow ass over here and let me give you a proper nightcap," she smirked rubbing on my dick.

I was exhausted, but she instantly had me ready to go another round. My little soldier was slowly stirring in my boxers. I looked around as she openly grabbed my hand and walked me into her apartment. I couldn't believe that Gia was about to let me smash while I was still wearing her best friend and her best friend's mother all over me. These bitches just didn't give a fuck anymore! The thirst was definitely real. I shook my head and thought about how this was going to be an extremely long night! Damn these good looks!

« Chapter 21 Glamma »

The Past "Alicia"

I KNOW EVERYONE IS sitting around thinking that I'm the dumbest chick to ever live. The truth is, I only decided to stay with Mike because I was terrified to leave. He had already proven that he would seriously hurt me if I decided to leave him. I feared for my safety as well as for the safety of my unborn child.

When he told me that if he couldn't have me no one would, I believed him. I could see the seriousness in his eyes. Since he came to my house that night to 'talk' he honestly has been trying to get us back on track. Of course, Cee Cee was not happy with my decision.

But as always, she supported my decision, but I was too embarrassed to tell her about him putting his hands on me that day. I could have told my mother, but again I was so ashamed. I did come around to finally telling her I was pregnant. I was ready for her to scream, yell and cry. But somehow, my mother already knew that I was knocked up.

After nervously telling her, she replied, "Alicia, you are my child. Did you seriously think that I wouldn't notice something like that? Your cycle comes a week before mine does. You haven't used any of your pads in over 3 months. And I've noticed your insatiable appetite. You've also put on a little weight in your midsection. Girl, I assess strangers for a living, so please know that I assess my kids too.

Never think for a second that just because I work a lot of hours, that I don't know what goes on in my house. I have eyes and ears everywhere. You're my daughter and I love you. I can't say that I'm not disappointed, however, what is done is done. There is nothing that I can say that will make you feel worse than you already do right now.

Terminating this baby is out of the question. He is our little miracle baby. But Lord! I am too young and fine to be someone's grandmother! Maybe I can be Nana or GiGi...or perhaps Mother the Sequel or Glamma. What do you think?!"

"My baby is about to have a baby!" She exclaimed emotionally.

"Mom, I am sooooo sorry that I allowed this to happen. I've always tried to make you proud of me. You don't hate me, do you?" I asked tearing up after my mom began to cry.

"Alicia there is nothing that you could EVER do to make me hate you. No one in this entire world is perfect. We all make mistakes. Hell, I wasn't much older than you when I had you. As a parent, you just want things to be easier for your children. I don't want you to ever know what it's like to struggle. How does Mike feel about your pregnancy? He does know, doesn't he?" She inquired.

"Yes ma'am, he knows. Honestly, he is very happy about me being pregnant. That fact alone has made this entire ordeal much more tolerable. I'm just so scared about the future. How will I be able to finish school and join the military.

I don't think they enlist unwed mothers. Everyone will judge me and look at me differently. I don't know if I can do this! What if I'm a terrible mother? Oh ma! Why did this happen to me?! We should've been more careful!" I cried.

"Girl hush, shit happens. You and I both know that everything happens for a reason. It is not up to us to know what God's plans are. Just know that he has one. You are destined to do great things, even with my grandson inside of you. This will only make you stronger. I hate that you have to grow up faster than you should, but know that I will always be here for you."

"Ma, that is the second time that you've referred to the baby as a "he". Why is that?"

"I've already told you Alicia, nothing happens in my home without me knowing about it. You are definitely having a boy. I can feel it."

"I love you so much ma. Thanks for being here for me. I truly appreciate everything that you do for us."

My mom stood up and gave me a tight hug. "I love you too Lee Lee. I will always have your back baby."

∞

I suppose one of the benefits to informing my mother of my pregnancy was that she treated me more like an adult. Mike was now able to stay over as he pleased. We didn't have to be as discreet as before. I still tried to be respectful and I never had sex while my mother and sisters were home.

I was now approaching the fourth month into my pregnancy and was scheduled to have an ultrasound the following week to find out the sex of the baby. Naturally, I wanted a girl to doll up. But my mom, Mike and Cee Cee were all convinced that I was having a boy. Trying to find the bright side of things, I knew that I would be happy just having a healthy baby.

Plus, if I had a boy first, he'd be able to protect his little sister, provided I chose to have more children later down the road. Much much later! Mike was back to his usual charming self. He catered to my every need. If I asked for pickle flavored ice cream at two in the morning, he would see to it that I got exactly what I wanted.

He was out boosting more, working to set money aside for us. Between Mike, my mom and my bestie, my baby was already set for a while. Of course, everything was blue or green. I was starting to pray for a boy now. I'd hate to have to return all the items they'd purchased over the last few months.

I had begun to soften up to Mike. I'd forgiven him and no longer feared him. He still continued to apologize for his previous behaviors, and I felt that he had redeemed himself. He'd give me spontaneous massages and bubble baths. I just wished that we were able to spend time together like we used to. I knew that he was out there hustling for us, so I tried to take it easy and not pester him too much.

I loved him and just wanted what was best for him...for us. I wanted us to be a family. I didn't want to be a single parent. I was performing well in school. I had stopped cheering because I didn't want to risk harming my baby. I'd substituted the cheering for walking, that way I still got adequate exercise. I didn't want to gain too much weight during this pregnancy.

I already felt big as a house. I prayed daily that I wouldn't get any stretch marks or hemorrhoids. They both grossed me out. Cocoa butter was my new best friend. I never scratched any of my itches, instead I'd rub some cocoa butter on those areas. So far it was working.

I had talked to both my mother and Mike about me finding a part-time job until I delivered the baby, but they were both adamantly against it. Cee Cee had told me that her job could use another cashier. Everyone treated me as if I were handicapped and incapable of performing any task that required physical labor. I was bored out of my mind!

The Sunday before my appointment to determine the sex of my baby, I was laying on the couch eating a peppermint infused pickle. I found myself bored as usual and there wasn't a damn thing on worth watching. My mom was working, Mike was out hustling, and the twins were at a sleepover. So, I decided to call Cee Cee. She and Eli had been spending so much time together that I hadn't seen much of her lately outside of school.

"Hey Bitch! You've forgotten all about my fat ass I see. You've kicked me to the curb and found you a new best friend!"

"Hey baby momma! You know it isn't even like that! I have missed you too. I've actually been on lockdown at home. My crazy ass parents had me locked in the damn basement. I was only allowed to go to school and work. They wouldn't let me use the phone for a week.

They were upset that I'd brought a B+ home and beat the brakes off me with an extension cord. To make matters worse, they saw that I was absent that one day when we went to the clinic. They kept asking me where I went, but apparently, none of my answers were good enough. I can't wait until I can move far away from their evil asses. I fucking hate my miserable life.

Why didn't they just abort me if they planned on doing me this way? No one deserves this. Why does God allow things like this to happen to good people? I go to church three times a week. I pray and I try to be good to everyone, yet I still suffer. Anyway, enough about me and my crappy life girl. How have you and my baby been?" Celeste asked after venting.

"Oh, Cee Cee, I am so sorry. I hate your fucking parents. I can't wait for you to get away from those assholes either. They are always walking around acting all holy and sanctified. Fucking hypocrites. They are both going straight to hell. I'm sorry that I got you in trouble. I should've known they'd overreact. I'm happy that you feel more comfortable talking about what's going on at home."

"Alicia, you don't have to apologize. I was where I was meant to be that day. You needed me and I wanted to be there for you. You're my family. To hell with them. Karma's a bitch. But anyway, enough about them. What's new with ya?"

"Baby daddy, I have been bored out of my mind! Everyone is treating me as if my legs and arms are broken. Don't get me wrong, at first it was really nice having everyone catering to me, but now I'm over it. I need to get out of this house!!! Let's do something! Anything!!!"

"What do you want to get into? I know your ass is hungry."

"Let's hit the mall up and do a little shopping. We can eat there too when we are done. I'll be by in 30 minutes to pick you up," I stated.

∞

"Cee Cee that dress looks so good on you! You should get it, but I think the red will really pop against your skin tone. My best friend is too fly!" I squealed loudly.

"I'm jealous because my big ass can't squeeze into nothing cute anymore! I cannot wait to have my body back!" I stated rubbing my belly.

I had tried on and purchased some maternity clothes. I had to give up on squeezing into my pre-pregnancy clothes. I bought five dresses, three pairs of maternity pants, five shirts and some panties.

While I didn't like the way the maternity clothes looked, I had to admit they fit much better than my clothes at home. Next, Cee Cee and I decided to grab a few pair of shoes. I was so happy for my friend. I loved seeing her finally wearing fashionable clothes. The fact that she could purchase the things on her own made it all that much sweeter.

I loved her with or without them, but I know she felt better with them. Her confidence level had drastically improved...despite the fuckery she endured at home. I had decided to keep it simple and got two pairs of comfortable sandals. I was done wearing my stilettos for now.

By the time Cee Cee had picked out her shoes, I was famished. We had decided that the food court would be our next pit stop, before continuing our little shopping spree. I knew for sure I was in need of a mani and pedi. We both decided that we wanted Chinese food.

After receiving our orders, we sat down and started laughing and having a great time. I was so happy that we were both able to escape and spend this time together.

"Cee Cee, you know that we are finding out what the sex of the baby is tomorrow, right? Do you think that you can make it? I scheduled it late, so that we wouldn't have to miss school," I asked.

"Alicia, you already know that I wouldn't miss it for the world. Even if it were during school hours. That beat down would be worth it baby momma."

"Awww, thank you baby daddy," I joked.

"Cee Cee lately I've been so lonely. My mom has been working like Kizzy Kinte and Mike has been on the block trying to sell extra clothes for me and the baby. I try not to bitch, but I wish he was at home more. He's always telling me that he can't make moves and get money by lying up under me all day. I get that but damn, I haven't physically seen his ass in two whole days.

His ass better make it to the appointment tomorrow or we are..." I stopped talking to focus in on what Cee Cee was glaring at with her mouth agape.

I followed her gaze to a very familiar person and my heart instantly shattered into a million pieces. I literally couldn't breathe and begin hyperventilating. Poor Cee Cee had to verbally calm me down and helped me reestablish a normal breathing pattern.

I looked on as the father of my unborn baby held up a beautiful baby girl that was his exact replica. She appeared to be about a month old. Trailing behind him was a very attractive petite woman who I assumed was the little girl's mother. I don't recall blinking or closing my mouth once as warm salty tears trickled down my face.

I could hear Cee Cee talking to me, yet I understood nothing. I was literally in a state of shock. The woman following Mike, didn't appear happy at all. I couldn't help but to wonder if she even knew about my existence. Did she know that Mike was in fact expecting another child in five months?

I had so many questions, but I was too devastated in that moment to investigate any of them. I wanted to put as much distance between me and that son of a bitch as humanly possible. I broke out of my trance and looked at Cee Cee.

"Get me the fuck out of here friend. Get me out of here!" I shouted.

Apparently recognizing my voice, Mike swiftly shifted his eyes in our direction. He looked as if he had seen a ghost. Somehow, I was able to see the color drain from his dark handsome face.

He looked as if he wanted to stop me as I ran with my worried friend in tow. He must not have wanted to make a scene in the mall...or around *his* daughter. Once we made it to my mom's car, I automatically sat in the passenger seat. I knew that I was mentally incapable of operating the car.

Had he brought his doggish ass out of the mall at that very moment, I would have had Cee Cee run him down. I could feel her staring at me, but I was too hurt to even acknowledge her at the moment. I didn't want her pity, yet it was written all over her face. He had played me yet again.

I felt so foolish. So humiliated. So gullible. So STUPID! Why couldn't this boy just do right? Why wasn't I enough to keep him from straying? I was beyond done and no amount of intimidation could change my mind this time. I had no fight left. I had tried to make it work for the baby, but screw that shit! I was prepared to die. As far as I was concerned, Mike had already killed me.

« Chapter 22 Pimping Ain't Easy »

The Past "Gladys"

SINCE LUKAS MURDERED Nate, we had essentially become inseparable. He had been showering me with lots of attention. He was so sweet and tender with me. He had practically become my family. He was at my house more often than he was at his own. I loved having him around. I'm not sure how I would have made it through the first few months following my father's death without his presence.

He was my knight in shining armor. The remainder of my senior year of high school was uneventful. I graduated at the top of my class. I had even been elected valedictorian. I was elated to have the opportunity to fill such big shoes. Lukas was there rooting for me as always in the audience.

It was all bittersweet. Deep down, I wished that my parents were also in the audience cheering me on. I knew they were both smiling down from heaven. They'd be proud of me. I had decided to overcome my hardships and make the best out of an extremely difficult situation. I could have made dozens of excuses as to why I shouldn't continue to pursue my goals, but I didn't find any that were good enough.

I wanted to be just like my father. I loved little ones and hoped to have my very own football team one day. I guess the apple doesn't fall far from the tree. My mother had also wanted a large family; unfortunately, she was unable to see it come to fruition.

I was now pursuing my dream of becoming an elementary school teacher at the University of Missouri-St. Louis (UMSL). I had opted to take on a super heavy load to obtain my degree faster. I was also still waitressing to cover my bills since I had opted to live off campus. I had plenty of money in my savings account, but I never wanted to touch it. I went to work and school every day as if I didn't have a penny to my name.

Thanks to Lukas, I was now the proud owner of a gently used Ford Focus. The car was not flashy; however, it served its purpose by getting me from point A to point B. I refused to allow him to spend a lot of money on a car for me. It just wasn't necessary. This had to be a huge weight lifted off Lukas. I knew that I had to be cramping his style. Since the attempted rape, he had been extremely overprotective. He didn't want me to go anywhere without him.

I had tried to convince him that I was a big girl on numerous occasions, but he simply wasn't having it. Although Lukas and I were spending a lot of time together, I knew that he was probably seeing other women. We never established that we were an item. He still hung around in the neighborhood. Lukas seemed to have ditched his harem, but that didn't mean anything.

I still didn't have the slightest idea about what he did for a living. My papa didn't raise a fool, so I knew that he was into illegal activities, I just wasn't sure which ones. I prayed for him a lot. I didn't know what I would do if something bad happened to him. Lately, I had begun to realize that I truly had feelings for Lukas.

I always assumed that the feelings were mutual. His actions showed me that he cared about me, but he never verbalized his feelings for me. He would introduce me to others' as his *"friend"* but would become enraged when other men showed an interest in me.

Lukas was well aware of the fact that I wanted to wait until I was married before having sex. He respected me and had never made a pass at me. I had seen some of the many women who usually surrounded him, and I knew he was probably sexing them, since I was being such a prude. He was sending me mixed messages and I needed clarity. One evening I decided to pick his brain after noticing our waitress giving us both the stink eye.

"Luke, do you have a girlfriend? And what is it that you do for a living? Hell, I don't even know if you have kids." I quizzed.

"G, you are so nosey woman. You work for the F.B.I now or something? Don't ask me things that you can't handle and that will hurt your feelings."

"Luke, you already know so much about me and my life, yet I hardly know anything about you. Aren't we friends? You never talk about yourself," I huffed in annoyance.

"We can discuss it later on down the road. You cannot handle my truths just yet."

"Seriously Luke? I can handle whatever you're willing to tell me. You can trust me. Please...."

"No, I don't have a girlfriend. I have females keep me company from time to time. I'm not sure if I can commit to just one woman to be honest with you. In regard to your question about kids, one of the women that I've been sleeping with is claiming that I am the father of her daughter.

I don't really believe it because she sleeps around and I've always strapped up. Despite all of this, I visit the little girl and give her mother money to help out. I'm a man and will always take care of my responsibilities," he admitted.

"The waitress...did you sleep with her? She keeps looking at me as if she wants to scratch my eyes out."

"G, come on..." He hesitated.

"I can handle it. Answer the question Luke!" I snapped.

"See, what you are not getting ready to do is yell at me. Yes! Yes! Yes! I fucked her. I've fucked a lot of women G! Are you happy now?!"

I knew that I had no right to be upset. He was not my man. He was practically a stranger. But that fact alone didn't make the sting from his admissions hurt any less. I stared down at my hands. I could feel his gaze burning into the top of my head as I found my will to speak again.

"So...so what do you do for a living?" I stammered.

"Well, I sell a little weed...and I assist women with finding short term dates while doubling as their security."

I allowed his words to marinate for a split second until I blurted out, "You're a pimp! A filthy, disgusting pimp! How could you?!"

"Gladys, calm down. It isn't what you think. I do not force any of them to sell their bodies. Every girl that works for me does it willingly. I'm not cruel to them. I do not beat them. I allow them time off and I even make sure that they all have healthcare. Not all *pimps* are like those assholes you see depicted in the movies. I run a respectable business." He proclaimed proudly.

"Suddenly, I'm not feeling well. If you wouldn't mind, I'd like to go home," I stated pushing my untouched food away.

This entire evening was a bust. I had found out that Lukas

was sleeping with numerous women, had commitment issues, had an illegitimate child out there, was a pimp and had banged the freaking waitress who was serving us. I wasn't crazy enough to eat anything she brought to our table.

Oh, and let's not forget that he sells a little weed. Sadly, that seemed so minor in comparison to all his other revelations tonight. I had a terrible migraine brewing. I needed air. And space. Blowing out an exasperated sigh, he threw his hands up defeated. I swiftly grabbed my purse and darted out of the restaurant. Once reaching his car, I was stopped by one of my classmates from school.

"Hello Gladys, what have you been up to?"

"Oh, hi Omar. I haven't been up to much besides school and work. All work and no play. You know me," I chuckled.

"How have you been? How's your English paper coming along? Mr. Morris doesn't play! I can't believe he actually wants our papers to be twenty-five pages long! That man hates us all and will be the death of me," I slid my index finger across my throat exaggeratingly.

Omar laughed in agreement before asking, "So who are you here with?" He glanced around before his eyes landed back on me.

"Nobody important," I responded looking into the restaurant's window. I noticed Lukas arguing with our waitress. He was so foul and disrespectful for that.

Not wanting to wait for their lover's quarrel to end, I asked, "Hey listen, would you mind giving me a lift home? I rode here with someone, but I don't want to be bothered with them anymore. I can give you gas money."

"Sure Gladys, I'd be glad to. Let me just go in and pick up my to go order. Oh, and keep your money woman." He beamed.

During the ride to my house, I had learned a great deal about Omar. We had never talked much in school, but I'd discovered that he was hilarious. He kept me laughing and was just the distraction that I needed to take my mind off Luke. I suppose I should have been more cautious about asking for a ride after I was nearly raped. However, I had to get away from Luke.

Besides, I was carrying my pepper spray and taser gun. Omar could get froggy if he wanted to! I was a little sad when we pulled up to my house. I wasn't ready for him to go. However, I knew we both had our papers to finish. Besides I didn't want to give Lukas the opportunity to catch up to us.

I could almost overlook all the things that he'd admitted to, except the fact that he was exploiting women in such a terrible manner. Moments like this made me hate the fact that I had given Luke a key to my house. I was so stupid. He never gave me a key to his damn house.

Come to think of it, I'd never even been to his house. We had always hung out over here. Why hadn't I noticed these things before now? It was time to end this one-way friendship. He simply had too many strikes against him. I was trying to become a schoolteacher and couldn't associate myself with people like him.

Twenty minutes after I had arrived home, I heard my front door opening. I knew it could only be one person. I walked into the living room to find Lukas sitting on the couch looking as if he had a lot on his mind.

"Look Lukas, I'm not really in the mood for company right now. So, can you please leave?" I asked as cordial as I could.

"I will leave after we talk about this. Why are you so bothered by what we discussed at the restaurant? You said that you could handle it."

"I'm not bothered. I told you that I'm not feeling well. So again, can you please just let yourself back out? Thanks," I lied.

"G, the truth is, I grew up around this shit. Hell, my own momma turned tricks for a few measly bucks and my father was apparently one of her johns. Don't you think I'd like to be doing something else with my life? This is all I know."

"Lukas, you are still young and could do anything that you set your mind to. I'm sorry, but as long as you are in the pimping business, we cannot be friends." I replied.

"I hear you and I respect your decision. I'm going to change. You'll see. I want better for myself. I'm not blind G. I know that you're digging me and just know I'm feeling you too. I haven't courted you, yet because I'm not the man you need right now. I will ask that you please have patience and wait for me. I'm coming for you when I get my shit together. Okay?"

I simply nodded as he planted a gentle kiss upon my forehead. A single tear streamed down my face as I watched my first crush walk out of my life.

« Chapter 23 Girl Next Door »

The Past "Lukas"

YOU MAY CALL ME Luke or Mr. Monroe. If you don't remember anything else about me, know that I am a man of my word. I had been working hard and making all kinds of moves both personally and professionally. I had plenty of money saved. I had decided to walk away from almost all of my illegal activities and opened my first laundromat.

While a part of me had made those moves to appease Gladys, I had already been thinking about leaving the game for a while now. She was just my motivation to implement my plans sooner. I had to glamourize what I did for a living, just a little bit. I couldn't divulge the truth of how truly deep I was in the game.

I was ruthless and had quickly excelled in this game. I was one of the most well-known pimps in St. Louis. My real money came from human trafficking. I'd never walk away from those funds. Truthfully, I didn't sell weed at all. There wasn't enough money in it for a businessman like me. I specialized in the distribution of cocaine and heroin. I was a jack of all trades and was making money hand over fist.

I had been watching Gladys for a while now. She was very beautiful and had a body that was guaranteed to turn a large profit. I simply couldn't decide what I wanted to do with her. I would turn a huge profit if I sold her directly into the trafficking business, but I knew how brutal that world was and didn't want her to experience such a fate. I honestly couldn't tell you why I cared so much.

I had never spared anyone from that life, especially if it meant dollars were walking away from my pockets. I had concluded after much consideration, that I'd have her work directly for me. It was me who had sold her father the heroin laced with rat poisoning and battery acid on the day he died.

I had also ensured that he'd received the purest work that I had on deck. If the nigga had to check out, at least he went with a bang. I knew he would greedily slam that entire bag of smack into his veins. The junkie fucker had administered enough heroin into his system to kill five grown men.

Mr. Berry had been my high school math teacher. I hated his punk ass to the core. He was a huge snitch who thought he was better than everyone else. His black ass didn't recognize that his shit stunk just like the rest of our asses. He was responsible for singlehandedly getting me suspended numerous times, which eventually led to my expulsion during my sophomore year of high school.

As I said before, I was making money hand over fist even while at school. His Uncle Tom ass had cost me a lot of business and for that, he had to pay. I wasn't a bad kid; I was just trying to survive. Life had served me lemons and all I wanted to do was make a little lemonade.

My mom was still hooking and jumping from nigga to nigga. She didn't have time for me. She did pay all the bills, but I was responsible for my own food and clothing. She felt that since she was barely at home, she was already being generous enough by paying the bills. I'm a patient man. I didn't seek out revenge against Mr. Berry instantly.

I knew that if I had retaliated right away, it would have been obvious who was behind the attack. I formulated a plan to make him one of my customers and to make his daughter work for me. Her pussy would replace all the money her father had cost me during my earlier years. Killing him would have been way to easy. I wanted him to suffer slowly before I snuffed him out. Years after Mr. Berry had me kicked out of school, the opportunity of a lifetime presented itself.

I had designated one of my girls, Thandie, to get the ball rolling. What I liked most about Thandie was the fact that she had more of a girl next door look. She was my wholesome bitch. You'd never in a million years believe that she was a hooker. The fact of the matter is, she was a beast in the pussy game. Her assignment was to seduce Mr. Berry at the annual school Christmas party.

She pretended to have a child that attended the high school. I watched from the crowd as she flirted and charmed the socks off of him. I could tell that he was enthralled in the rehearsed conversation.

Thandie was a natural beauty and I felt that she somewhat resembled the picture of his late wife. He used to always have a picture of her and a picture of Gladys on his desk. I always thought they were both gorgeous.

Thandie's job was to earn his trust and to eventually start offering him weed laced with cocaine. She was initially met with some resistance. However, after I beat her ass near extinction, she had finally spit the right game to him and he tried it. After daily smoke sessions for approximately a week, Mr. Berry was hooked. He fell fast and hard for coke. His bitch ass was a natural.

It was as if he were born just to be one of my fiends. He

had quickly ditched the weed and sought out straight cocaine. Initially he'd just smoke and snort it. I sat back and watched his rapid demise. Once he was hooked on cocaine for about a year, I had Thandie introduce him to a little heroin. I could've upgraded him sooner, but I was having way too much fun.

The drugs were all on the house in the beginning. My charitable contributions to Mr. Berry had me feeling like a God. Now that I had his rat ass hooked, he was being charged like all the rest of my Lukettes. Soon he had ditched the cocaine and went to shooting heroin. He was a full-fledged junkie. My mission was accomplished. I had his snitching ass eating out of the palm of my hand.

It filled me with absolute joy the first time that I had the opportunity to serve him directly. He looked embarrassed for a slight moment. He even went as far as to lecture me on how he had higher hopes for me and that his intentions always came from a good place. Blah, blah, blah! I had quickly ended his afterschool special sounding ass.

"Look bitch, are you here to conduct business or not? You are holding up my fucking line. I must say, I am proud that you've decided to join my team. You are now considered one of my Lukettes. That's how I refer to all of *my* base heads. If there is ever anything, I can do for you, let me know. You know where to find me," I grinned showcasing my straight white teeth.

"And I do mean anything, Mr. Berry."

After servicing him, I knew it was only a matter of time before he would start seeking handouts. His appetite for heroin had grown substantially. He wouldn't be able to meet his growing dependence on the drug for much longer. I would remain patient and make my move only when the time was right.

Still, I wasn't quite satisfied yet. He hadn't quite hit rock bottom. He still had his little teaching job for the moment. However, I knew his days there were coming to an end. I was almost tempted to place an anonymous call to the school board to have him drug tested. However, that would make me no better than his snitching ass.

I would allow him to shoot himself in the foot...so to speak. I was so proud of Thandie's handiwork that I paid for her to go on a month long, all-expense paid vacation to the Bahamas. I'm sure her overly used puss needed a little time to air out. Besides, I felt a little guilty about whooping her ass the way that I did. I never had to lay hands on her before.

Eventually I learned through my sources that Mr. Berry had finally lost his job. Apparently, his attendance was lacking, and his behaviors were erratic. They didn't automatically terminate him. They gave him several warnings and numerous opportunities to get himself clean. I had to give credit where credit was due, he had tried a few times.

There would be periods when I wouldn't see him for a week or so. But like all my other faithful addicts, he would always come running back. He never came to me short, up to that point. However, after he lost his job, that was a different story. I know it killed him to have to beg me for a hit.

And you better believe, my petty ass made him beg like Keith Sweat too! But I always gave it to him. Next time he'd have to put in work for my product. This was not the Ronald McDonald house anymore. I didn't hand out charity...at least not after I had already turned you out.

I needed money, electronics or you had to put in some work. After tossing the small bag at his forehead, he quickly bent down to retrieve it and ran out of my trap. I felt so powerful in that moment. I had won a major victory!

« Chapter 24 The Escape Clause»

The Past "Celeste"

SHOCKED DOES NOT EVEN began to describe how I felt when Eli came up to my job and took me out to lunch. I was even more shocked when he bought me a brand-new BMW. I have been on cloud nine ever since. Of course, I had to concoct a believable story about how I could afford such an expensive car to my parents.

I simply told them that it was an early graduation gift from Ms. Trina. They didn't look as if they liked the idea, but after talking to Ms. Trina, she was somehow able to convince them to allow me to keep it. She had told them that she had also bought Alicia one. My dad was home a lot less than he used to be and my mother continued to isolate to her room after work.

I wasn't sure what was going on between the two of them, but I suspected that the outcome was not going to turn out favorably. I just tried to distance myself from them both as much as possible. I wanted to remain as far away from their radar as possible.

I tried to avoid setting either of them off at all costs. The day that I had to ask Joe if I could leave early truly upset me. Joe was not happy that I had a boyfriend, although he had initially agreed to keep our relationship professional. He seemed insulted that I had chosen Eli over him. I reminded him that he was married with children. I also reminded him that he was too old for me.

"Celeste, I know we agreed to keep it professional, however, I can't get you out of my head. I really do care about you. I can't explain it. I know I have a lot to lose, but I simply have to have you. I told you before that my wife and I are not on great terms.

I'll be leaving her soon and then we can be together. Call me selfish, but I want you. I have to have you. I can't stand to see you with that clown. I know you're too young for me. But we can keep us a secret until the time is right. What do you say, beautiful?"

Joe walked over to me and traced the outline of my lips with his index finger. His lustful gaze had me paralyzed. Not wanting to back down I maintained eye contact with him. His lips then covered mine. My first instinct was to slap fire to his cheek, however, his touch felt amazing. Almost hypnotic. I felt so confused...yet aroused.

He must have noticed too, and before I realized it, my engorged right nipple now resided in his warm moist mouth. A sultry moan escaped my lips. The exaggerated slurping noises he was making caused my panties to instantaneously become drenched. He smelled so amazing and his touch felt so right.

Just as Joe was about to slide his hand into my pants, the gleam from his gold wedding band snapped me out of my lustful stupor. Realizing what I had allowed to happen made me angry with myself. I should've stopped him.

Now I had just made things between us even more complicated. Slapping his hand away from my open zipper, I roughly pushed him away from me. I then readjusted my breasts inside of my bra. We stared at each other for what seemed like hours, before I briskly left out of his office.

A million thoughts were running through my mind as the reality of the situation sunk in. I couldn't believe that I had just fooled around with my married boss while my boyfriend was in the next room. Damn, I was a hoe! I was so embarrassed. As Eli came into view, I tried to act as normal as I possibly could.

I attempted to appear unbothered. Of course, Eli was pretty good at reading me by this point. He knew that something was wrong with me. Thoughts of coming clean had crossed my mind...but I didn't want to lose him. I loved him. I don't know what came over me in Joe's office. I was possessed.

∞

When Eli stated that he was going to get me a car, I felt lower than I ever had in my life. I knew that I didn't deserve his generosity. However, my shitty parents didn't raise a fool. After Eli and I parted ways, I couldn't wait to show my best friend my new car.

I never wanted to leave my car. I'd sleep in it if I could get away with it! Pulling up in front of Alicia's house, I decided to be extra and lay on my horn. After a couple of minutes, I saw Alicia peep out of her living room window. That was soon followed by her coming out of her front door.

"Heifer, what ever happened to good old-fashioned knocking? You're lucky that I love you, otherwise I'd have to kick your ass for interrupting my nap. You know this baby makes me crabby if I miss my naps. And whose car is this?! It is nice!" She exclaimed, nodding her head approvingly.

"It's *my* car girl!!! Eli bought it for me this morning. He said that he didn't want me to have to rely on other people to get around anymore. I think he might be the one best friend!" I shrieked.

"Unh unh! Cee Cee, girl stop lying! Whose ride is this for real, for real?" She asked doubtfully.

Instead of responding, I reached over her and pulled out all the documents in my glove compartment. I then silently handed them over for her to read. I watched her from my peripheral vision. She glanced at the paperwork, then at me.

She repeated her goofy charade three times before she screamed, "Oh my God! My girl is pushing a B.M.W!!! Ahhh! You know you have to give Eli some pussy now, right? That nigga has earned the right to at least slip the tip in!"

I burst out laughing at her silly ass. I shook my head and replied, "Ewwww! You are so damn nasty! Alicia, I told you what happened when I stopped by his place. I let him eat me out and was prepared to go all the way, but he just stopped all of a sudden. He didn't want to have sex with me. Maybe he didn't like my body. I have been putting on some weight now that I have my own income and can eat whenever I want."

"Bitch please, Eli's horny ass wanted to fuck. Has it ever crossed your mind that he actually respects you and wants your first time to be special? Isn't that what he told your hard-headed ass? Stop always thinking the worse. Everything happens for a reason. Who knows, had you gone all the way you could be standing in my shoes right about now. It'll happen when the time is right. Don't force it honey," She replied before hugging me. Her words alleviated me of all my insecurities.

"Besides, maybe he stopped because your coochie stank or something," she teased. I giggled and rolled my eyes at her retarded ass.

"Girl, anyway! How's my baby doing baby mama?" I inquired rubbing her protruding belly.

"The baby is great baby daddy. I'm not experiencing morning sickness anymore thank God! I can't wait to find out what I'm having so that we can start picking out names. Plus, yall's asses keep buying all this blue and green shit. I could be having a girl, ya know?"

"Bitch, you are not having a damn girl! When will you get with the program, heifer? That's my nephew in there. Have you seen or heard from Mike since the mall incident?" I quizzed.

"Girl, hell no! Fuck Mike! And I'm not trying to hear or see his ass either! I don't have time for the lies. Cee Cee, he played me so good...twice! There will NOT be a third. He most certainly deserves a round of applause for those Oscar winning performances he performed for me.

I will never trust another nigga again. He didn't even have the decency to strap up before he fucked the bitch. Or...oh no! Cee Cee...am I the side bitch, since she had him first?! I hate his black ass so much for this!!!" She emotionally exclaimed.

"Calm down girl, you're going to stress my baby out. Like you said, fuck Mike! I have your back and so does your mother. I'll babysit whenever you need me to. We will figure this out. Okay?" I asked gently nudging her left shoulder with my own.

"I hear you. This is just not how I imagined my high school years going, ya know? I did finally tell my mom. I know she is disappointed, but she tried not to show it. She was very supportive. I feel like such a fool. It seems like everyone knows and is laughing at my naivety and stupidity. I just want to hide under a rock sometimes."

I tilted my head to look at her. "Who is talking right now?! Since when have you ever given two shits about what these nosey ass fuckers thought about you? They don't know a thing about you. Let them talk. Screw them!" I countered.

"Yeah, you're right best friend. I'm going to continue to do me. I'm not getting ready to let them or Mike's funky ass stress me or my baby out. I'm over it all."

∞

The following week I avoided Joe like the plague. I was too ashamed to even make eye contact with him and didn't trust myself to be alone with him. He seemed to be somewhat distant as well. I just assumed that he felt bad about what had transpired as well. I hated keeping this from Eli, however, I didn't see how confessing would help our budding relationship.

I thoroughly enjoyed his company. I craved the affection he showed me both in and out of school. Deep down I knew that I loved him, but was afraid to admit it even to myself. He had become my *second* best friend, second to Alicia of course.

He became my safe haven and I often imagined a future that included him. I hoped that he felt the same about me. But why was I also drawn to Joe?

It was as if God himself came to me with a simple solution to my dilemma. The owner of Divas R US was branching out and was nearing the completion of his second clothing store. I was going to ask for a transfer in order to get away from Joe.

Luckily for me, the manager of that store was a woman. Soon all my work-related matters would be a thing of the past. I didn't know how to approach Joe with my desire to transfer, but I knew that it had to be done. I couldn't continue to play this cat and mouse game. Not at Eli's expense. I just couldn't risk losing him.

We were playing a dangerous game and I wanted to distance myself from it all. We had a company picnic coming up in a few days. I figured that would be the perfect opportunity for me to hand over my transfer request to Joe. There would be a lot of people around and very little privacy to go into depth about the situation. I'd cited the distance as my primary reason for wanting to transfer. Joe and I of course would know better.

∞

I had invited both Alicia and Eli, but neither of them could attend the picnic. Alicia wasn't feeling well, and Eli had some business to tend to on the streets. I wasn't too disappointed about it. I still had my work friends to hang out with. I hadn't told them about my transfer request yet. I wanted to wait until it was approved first. Call me superstitious, but I didn't want to jinx myself. I never counted my chickens before they hatched.

On the day of the picnic, I decided to wear something casual and simple. I wore some white form fitting shorts with a red backless shirt. My feet were adorned in red gladiator sandals. I had just snuck and painted my finger and toenails white. My hair was straightened into a layered wrap. Since it was hot out, I had opted not to wear any makeup. I did apply some cherry scented lip gloss to my full lips.

As soon as I pulled up to the park, I noticed my coworkers Nivea, Angelika and Tyra huddled together on a nearby bench. They appeared to be laughing and having a great time.

As I approached them, I heard Nivea yell, "There goes my bitch right there! Hey boo!"

I blushed because she was extremely loud, and this was a work-related picnic. It was obvious that she had already consumed her fair share of alcohol. I greeted each woman with a warm hug and a smile. I then sat down, and we began to people watch and gossip. Tyra informed us that she was in the process of leaving her no good boyfriend once and for all. He lacked ambition and rarely held a job for longer than a month. To top it off, he had the audacity to be unfaithful. She was a good woman and deserved much much better.

She was a cute chocolate sister who I thought resembled Keshia Knight Pulliam. She didn't have to settle but she did because of her two kids. She was raised in a two-parent household and wanted the same for her offspring. Hell, as far as I was concerned, his punk ass was just another offspring. He didn't contribute to her household at all. I was happy to hear that she had finally put him out and changed her locks. He was such a loser.

Angelika was a lesbian and had sworn off men a long time ago. She was absolutely gorgeous, so I knew men hated that she wanted nothing more to do with them. She was what they called a soft stud. She would come to work one day looking like a Sanaa Lathan and then the next day she'd look like Monica from the movie Love and Basketball.

Either way she was breathtaking. She and her girlfriend Trinity had been going steady for a couple of years now. Angelika and Trinity were both twenty-five and had decided that they wanted to expand their family. They were looking for a sperm donor to help make their dream come true.

Angelika's stories were always hilarious. She'd often joke about how she fucked Trinity better than the guys fucked her. She was going to be the one to carry the baby. She would tell us how she and Trinity would meet random guys at clubs on the days she ovulated.

She would have one-night stands and send them on their merry way hoping that they conceived a baby. We would always yell at her for this. It wasn't safe playing Russian Roulette with these random guys. After about six months of meeting strange men, she finally decided to try a sperm bank. She joked that she just couldn't take the wack sex anymore.

After grabbing some food and drinks for ourselves, we begin to eat our food. I finally spotted Joe with who I presumed were his wife and kids. I nervously retrieved my transfer request form from my back pocket as I noticed them walking in our direction.

When they reached our table, I couldn't help but to feel a twinge of jealousy. Joe's wife, Mia, was so pretty. Her photos did her no justice. Why would he ever want to cheat on a woman as beautiful as she was. She was chubby and could stand to lose a few pounds, but her face was flawless.

Joe greeted each of us by name before he introduced us to each of his kids and his wife. She appeared to be extremely happy. I noticed that her smile reached her eyes as she looked lovingly at her husband.

Her wedding ring was blinding. This didn't match the story that he'd given me about them being unhappily married or about them being in an open relationship. She didn't appear to be the type of woman who was okay with sharing her man.

It is what Joe announced next that made my heart skip a beat.

"Ladies, I'm sure that you've heard about the other store opening soon. My wife, Mia, will be running that store out there. I wanted to ask if any of you were interested in working overtime? She could really use some help getting things set up. I've already bragged about how amazing you all are.

We would both be very appreciative for any assistance you could give us. She has already hired more than *enough* staff, however none of them are familiar with the Divas R Us layout. I'd like it if you could show them the ropes," he stated with a snide smirk as his eyes locked on mine.

While my coworkers hurriedly jumped on the opportunity to kiss ass and pick up the overtime, I slowly ripped up my transfer request. My mind was racing a mile a minute. How in the fuck did he know that I wanted to transfer?! I hadn't even told anyone. I refused to jump from the frying pan and into the fire.

I couldn't work with this man's wife every day knowing what had gone down between us. I could never pretend to be that fake around her. While everyone continued to chat, I lowly excused myself from the group. As I speed walked to my car, a chill ran through me. Glancing behind me, I nearly pissed on myself as I noticed both Joe and Mia glaring at me.

"What the hell was that about?! Weird ass fuckers," I mumbled to myself as I got into my car and sped off.

« Chapter 25 Vampire »

Present Day "Autumn"

AS DON HAD PREDICTED, I did become pregnant after only three months of us having sex. He kept his word and took me to get "rid" of the problem immediately. In no way, shape or form did I want a baby with him, however I silently grieved for the baby I had murdered. I know in my heart of hearts that we had made the right decision, but it didn't erase the pain and emptiness that I felt inside.

My innocent baby did not deserve such a violent fate. After the abortion, I told Don that I would not give him one more whiff of my pussy until my sister was brought to live with us once and for all. I was tired of playing his bullshit games, yet seeing no results. The abortion had truly changed me, and it was time for that fat fuck to hold up his end of the bargain.

He left me alone for a few weeks after the abortion. I guess he called himself giving me time to heal. Time to grieve. Nearly every day for the past three months he was buried balls deep inside of me, until this three-week reprieve. I was so relieved, and my body desperately needed to recuperate.

I was so stressed out. The day after my abortion, I was so depressed and was having the darkest of thoughts. The most unimaginable circumstances always seemed to infiltrate my tortured existence. I went on every single day with a bright, yet phony smile. No one ever knew the wiser.

At school, all of my classmates appeared to be so happy. Internally I envied all of their happy asses. I often wondered if their happiness was real or if it were made of silicone like mine. Were they being molested on a nightly basis? Had any of them witnessed either of their parents being murdered? Did they know what it was like to practically raise their younger siblings? Had any of them had their baby scraped from their wombs?

Most nights I prayed for normalcy. I just wanted to be ordinary. Genuinely happy. I know God doesn't give us more than what we can handle. However, at times I felt as if everything was going to collapse around and underneath me. I was slowly suffocating.

I wanted to numb the pain. So, I grabbed the box cutter that I had snagged from the junk drawer in the kitchen. I released the sharp blade from its protective sheath. I then stared blankly at the pointed blade. I proceeded to lift my nightgown and delivered four swift cuts to my right inner thigh. It hurt so good! I went from feeling absolutely nothing to instant euphoria.

Since my mother's untimely death and Don's relentless sexcapades, my cutting frequency had doubled. I have been in a constant state of pain and cutting was my only outlet. I had been cutting for years, but only when things became extremely stressful at home. My mom had been too busy chasing her next high to ever notice that I was a cutter.

The only people that knew were Wintress and now Don, by default. My sister always hated when I'd cut my flesh. She was perhaps the only person that could calm my nerves in highly stressful situations. She had prevented me from cutting more times than I can count. However, she was not here now to be my voice of reason. I was all alone.

Don also offered to get me professional help. I refused because I knew the only reason that he feigned concern was because he claimed my cutting turned him off. I suppose my rough keloids weren't his cup of tea. I told him that I had a great solution for his disdain. He could leave me the hell alone and focus on his little girlfriend instead. I didn't ask for this.

My eyes closed involuntarily as I felt warm blood began to trickle down my right medial thigh. Its warmth sent a calming sensation all over my body. In that moment, I felt that everything would be okay. I felt no emotional or physical pain, yet I was numb to happiness too. With my eyes still closed, I reached between my thighs.

With my index finger, I swiped a copious amount of my blood. I then placed my blood clad finger in between my teeth and cheek. I savored my blood's sweet, coppery taste for a few moments. Hearing a barely audible creak of the wooden floor caused my eyes to snap open.

My heart sank as I noticed four terrified eyes staring back at me with their mouths agape. In an instant, my feelings of numbness disappeared. The pain from the cut was overwhelming. As I tried to get up to comfort my foster brothers and reassure them that I was okay, I noticed for the first time that my cuts were continuing to bleed profusely. I had never seen that much blood after one of my cutting episodes.

I felt woozy, but I needed to get to the kids who were still staring at me from the doorway.

As I made it to my feet, I heard Chris scream, "Vampire!!!"

I watched as Landon signed the same thing with his shaky fingers. Weakly I tried to assure them that I was not a vampire, but as I got closer to them, they fled from the doorway. I heard Chris continuing to yell that I was a vampire. Too weak from the amount of blood I had lost, I collapsed to the floor.

I was dying and I welcomed it. I had no fight left in me. I didn't want to fight this fight anymore. Life was too hard. I longed to be with my mother again. I sent God a prayer asking him to protect Wintress. A couple of tears escaped my eyes before I could stop them. I rolled onto my right side so that I could expire with my dear sister being the last image that I saw before changing life forms.

"I'm ready for you God," I announced before succumbing to the wave of exhaustion that consumed me.

∞

In a panic, I opened my eyes still shaken up a bit from the nightmare I'd just had. The dream had seemed so real. I couldn't believe that I had been selfish enough to have contemplated leaving my sister here with absolutely no one. I didn't want to live and felt that I'd be better off dead, however, I would never leave my sister.

Feeling the urge to urinate, I attempted to sit up. As I sat up, excruciating pain stopped me in my tracks. It was then that I realized that I had a padded dressing on my right inner thigh. It was starting to seep through a little. Glancing around, I noticed that I had blood and IV fluids infusing. What the fuck happened to me? I thought to myself. The clearing of Don's thick throat made me roll my eyes in his direction.

"Autumn, what in the fuck were you thinking?! Were you trying to kill yourself? It took me hours to calm the boys down and convince them that you were not a vampire. They told me that they saw you drinking your own blood in here. What is going on?"

"Do I need to take you back to the hospital with the other crazies?"

"I had to call in some very expensive favors to have you discreetly treated here at home. If the state or your case manager finds out about this shit, they will remove you from this house. Is that what you want? They will put you back onto a psych ward and put you in a straitjacket. So, this better be a onetime deal."

"My mother doesn't need to know about this either. It will only add to the stress she already has. If you ever pull some shit like this again, I will get your sister and adopt her. I would then make sure that you never see her again. Just remember that shit you ungrateful little bitch!"

I believed everything that he had just said. I knew that I had gone way too far this time. I would make an effort to find better coping strategies. I couldn't jeopardize not having my little sister live with us. Or possibly having Don use her the way he used me. I promised Don that I would not cut anymore.

I still refused to see a psychiatrist about my demons. I figured I would get past my issues on my own. I just needed Wintress here and I would feel complete. Although I did agree not to cut anymore, I remained firm with Don when it came to my sister.

I refused to have sex with him again until my sister came home. Don knew that I was serious about me ending our little freaky arrangements, if he didn't bring my sister home immediately.

Shortly after I had cut Don off sexually, I overheard him talking to the Price family regarding them handing over Wintress. After they went back and forth, I had concluded that Don was paying $35,000 to get my sister. I couldn't believe that he was willing to pay that amount for a little girl that he'd only met once.

One thing for sure, I missed my little sister like crazy! I knew that she and the boys would hit it off. I talked about her all the time. Although I had grown to love them to pieces over the past few months, they just weren't Wintress. Eavesdropping on Don's phone call to the Prices had me cheesing from ear to ear.

That night when he crept into my bedroom, I didn't give him any attitude or resistance whatsoever. In fact, I felt that he deserved my body...he had finally earned the right to feel my inner velvety walls. As I expertly rode him into a state of delirium, I felt my usually dry vagina spew a little dew in his honor.

He most definitely noticed and thanked me by smacking me on my ample ass. I played his little game and moaned as if he was truly doing some damage with his little frail pink pecker. At times, I wondered if it would survive some of the rough sex fests that he insisted that we have every day. Aside from our nocturnal escapades, Don treated me very well. There was nothing that I would ask for that he would deny me.

I was old enough to know that what we were doing was wrong, but what other choices did I have? I could end things and potentially never see my sister again. Or I could continue and live the life that I'd always dreamt of having. Plus, as an added bonus, I'd soon have my little sister by my side.

I never knew that sex was so powerful and could control so many aspects of a persons' life. My body was a small sacrifice to ensure that my future remained bright. I spoke to Wintress every day and we'd been able to visit each other a couple times a week. The most difficult part was leaving and knowing that she'd be going to another home. She always cried when our visits concluded, and it would break my heart to pieces.

I liked my new school a lot more than my last one. I got along well with my classmates and had made quite a few friends. Wintress and I were often teased back in my old neighborhood because we never wore nice clothes. I had usually kept to myself and didn't have any friends. Now, it seemed as if everyone was drawn to me. I couldn't help but wonder if clothes truly made that big of a difference. That was the only thing that had changed about me.

I was performing well in school and was placed into honor's English classes. I enjoyed writing and looked up to my English teacher, Mrs. Norwood. She was a heavyset African American woman with the warmest smile. She always encouraged me in class and made me feel as if anything were possible.

She had told me that she saw something extraordinary in me. Mrs. Norwood thought that I was destined for greatness. I found her easy to talk to. She knew that my mother had been murdered. Sometimes I would tell Mrs. Douglas that I had group projects to avoid having to go straight home. Despite my efforts, Don never allowed me to spend the night out with my newly acquired friends.

It was in my honor's class where I met a timid girl named MaDonna. She was quiet and standoffish. She awkwardly avoided eye contact with everyone. I often found myself staring at her wondering why she acted the way that she did. What was her story?

After a group assignment was assigned one day, I approached MaDonna and asked her if she'd like to be my partner for the assignment. She shyly glanced around as if she thought that I was speaking to someone else.

I shook my head, chuckled and pointed at her. "I'm talking to you. It's MaDonna right?" I inquired already knowing her name.

"Uh uh, yes. My name is MaDonna Williams. And you're Autumn Monroe. It's nice to officially meet you," she curtly replied reaching out to shake my hand.

"You are correct. That is my name. Now, would you like to be my partner? I repeated.

I looked her over and realized that although we both attended this ritzy school, she appeared as if she came from my old neighborhood. I wondered if that is what drew me to her. She reminded me a little of myself prior to moving in with the Douglas family.

Her clothes appeared to be clean, however, she always appeared disheveled and wrinkled. Her hair was brushed back into its usual ponytail. She had a unique beauty that I knew she wasn't even aware that she had. Her striking eyes put me in the mindset of Erykah Badu. Her other features were simple, yet alluring.

Her clothes were baggy, and her shoes were scuffed. For some reason, all I wanted to do was help her.

"Um okay. I guess so. We can work on this assignment together. Or I can just do it and say that we worked on it together. That is what most of my past partners did. I don't mind. It must be done anyway. I'm sure you have more important things to focus on," she replied with a defeated shrug.

"MaDonna, that isn't why I asked to do the assignment with you. I'm capable of holding my own weight. I didn't make it into that class by cheating. Let's meet tomorrow in the library so that we can go over the details, okay?"

"Oh, before I forget, here is my number. Call me if you have any questions." I stated sliding her a piece of paper with my number written on it.

"That sounds like a plan. I will see you tomorrow Autumn," she replied before taking off down the hall.

Once she disappeared, I shook my head wondering who this MaDonna character was. Shaking off my strange new partner I headed towards the chauffeured driver that Don insisted that I have. I had tried to get him to buy me a car, but he'd refused. He didn't want me to have that level of independence. I knew he just wanted to keep tabs on me by any means necessary.

∞

MaDonna and I had done a wonderful job on our project. She was still mysterious to me, but she did open up a little. I had learned that she lived in south St. Louis City and was bused to our school because of her exceptional grades. She had four younger siblings. While she and two of her siblings lived with her grandparents, the other two lived with their dad. Her mother was in a terrible motor vehicle accident that left her a quadriplegic.

MaDonna's grandparents tried to care for their daughter and their five grandchildren, but it all proved to be too much. Neither of them was in the best of health themselves. MaDonna's mother, LaTonya, had married and divorced twice. She had three kids with her first husband and two with her second. LaTonya had been a terrific provider to her children. She had been the administrator of a long-term care facility. She'd been making well over a six-figure salary before her unfortunate accident. LaTonya's savings quickly dwindled away to nothing to help pay for her mounting medical expenses.

Luckily, LaTonya's second husband stepped up to the plate and took in his two children. MaDonna's father agreed to pay child support, but had no relationship with his children. While the child support helped a little, it wasn't nearly enough to support the three remaining kids. MaDonna's father had been the maintenance man at the long-term care facility in which she had worked. He wasn't making much to begin with.

MaDonna claimed that while her grandparents didn't have many material things, she was happy with them. There was always food and lots of love. My heart went out to my new friend. Why did good people always have to suffer? She didn't deserve this. Since MaDonna was about my size...give or take a curve of two, I'd given her some of my clothes and shoes. She had certainly begun to blossom.

She had become my first true friend aside from Wintress. Sure, I now had lots of *associates*, but none of them were real. I knew that none of them would've given me a second glance at my last school. MaDonna was humble and she was very real.

« Chapter 26 Papa's Putting In Work »

The Past "Lukas"

LIFE WAS FULL OF surprises, you know? I continued to pump Mr. Berry full of Missouri's finest smack, while keeping a watchful eye on his sexy ass daughter. By this time, homeboy was looking rough. These streets were even talking about how Mr. Berry had completely fell off. I must say, that nigga had integrity. Despite losing his job, he refused to steal things from his own house to support his drug habit.

Had I been a different type of man, I would've pitied him. But fuck that muthafucking snitch! About a week ago he came into my trap looking for some work. His usually lined up beard was now unkempt and decorated with unruly grey hairs.

"Hey what's up Luke man. How you doing, son?"

"Bitch, you ain't my daddy. What can I do for you B?"

"Look man, I need a favor. Can you hook me up and I'll come back through later on once I hit a lick? I'm hurting man."

"Nigga this isn't a charity house. I need money for my product. What the fuck I look like nigga?"

"Oh, come on Luke, don't be like that. You know I'm good for it man. Don't I always come through? Me and my buddy Lance have something lined up for later and I promise, you will be the first person I break off once we finish. Just help me out just this once!" He pleaded with panic in his voice.

"Yo Mr. B, you remember when I told you that I needed money, collateral or for you to put in work for my product? Well, you're in luck. I have some work for you. Then I'll hook your crackhead ass up. Deal? You can take it or leave it. I really don't give a fuck what you decide to be honest. But there are no more handouts my nigga. I'm sick of your freeloading ass." I replied cooly.

"Alright, alright, Youngblood. What job do you need me to do? Can you just bump me off first? I'm jonsing so bad that I can't even think straight."

"What muthafucking job do you know that pays up front? You will get your hit when the job is done. Now are you ready to shut the fuck up and listen?!"

"I'm all ears man." He mumbled.

"Good, follow me to the back real quick," I ordered.

After we reached my "makeshift" office, I turned and snarled at Mr. Berry. I watched him nervously shift from side to side as I continued to stare at him. The amount of hatred that I had for this man had me ready to blow his fucking brains out. Anticipation was etched in his face. The power that I had over him literally had my dick hard.

Unfastening my pants, I looked at Mr. B and said, "The job I have for you is simple. I want you to suck my dick. Not only do I want you to suck my dick, but I want you to suck this muthafucka better than anyone else has before. I need to get this nut off and I think you're the perfect nigga for that job."

I pulled out three bags of work and dangled them in front of him while I started to stroke myself.

"One bag is for you sucking my dick. The second one is if I cum and the last…is if you give me the best head I've ever had. I'm gonna need you to make up your mind fast, because I don't have all day to play with you. This work will last you for days…" I coaxed.

"Boy, I'm not on that faggot shit! Give me another job to do. I will rob and beat anyone's ass that you want me to. But I ain't getting ready to suck your muthafucking dick nigga! I'm a man damn it!" He angrily proclaimed.

"Alright then fuck it! Suit yourself, dumbass. Unfortunately, I don't have any other jobs today. I guess these will be waiting for you after you hit that lick with Lance," I said pulling my pants back up.

"Fuck man! Come on! Don't do this to me. Have a heart Youngblood. Help me! I'm begging you!" He pleaded as his voice cracked.

"Nigga, I've already told you what I wanted. Take it or leave it!" I barked.

My dick jumped as Mr. Berry slowly walked over to me with a blank expression on his face. Kneeling down on his knees, he was eye to eye with my erection. I could feel his rage piercing through me. He wanted to kill me, but was powerless to do so. I planned to break his ass down until he prayed for me to kill him.

Clearing my throat, I grabbed my dick and slapped his ass in the face with it. "Hurry up muthafucka. My shit is still bone dry. Wet this muthafucka up! I told your funky ass I didn't have all day. For a nigga who is wanting a hit, you sure are moving slow as fuck! Here sniff this shit real quick."

I handed him a small bag that contained cocaine and waited until he made the contents disappear.

He then glanced up at me and said, "No one can ever find out about this shit Youngblood...especially my daughter. Please keep this shit between us!"

"No problem. Now earn this work!"

With that, I felt his hesitant lips wrap around my throbbing member. As he awkwardly sucked me off, I begin to pump in and out of his mouth. Growing tired of him sucking my shit at a snail's pace, I grabbed him by the back of his head. I then begin to drill the fuck out of his mouth. At least his punk ass was smart enough to know not to use teeth. I glanced at the dingy mirror that was positioned to my left and enjoyed watching my ass muscles tense up only to relax again.

His technique needed lots of improvement, however, his suction was strong, and I was loving it. He kept his eyes closed throughout the entire ordeal, so he never noticed the smug expression that was plastered over my face. Seeing my anaconda occasionally poke at his cheek was a sight for sore eyes. I never in a million years thought that I'd be fucking the shit out of my old teacher's face.

I had this muthafucka gagging on my big ass tool, as I harshly pounded away at his face. I didn't give a fuck though. Fuck this nigga and his snitching ass throat. I was trying to destroy his larynx, so he'd be unable to snitch on anyone ever again. Finally getting tired of his gagging ass, I painted his throat with my special seeds.

Mr. B appeared to be in another world. Almost as if he were having an outer body experience. I guess he was still trying to come to terms with the fact that I just had my big ass dick in his mouth.

I devilishly looked at him and said, "Wow Mr. Berry, who would've thought that your head game was strong like that! I'm impressed. Shit, you should be proud of yourself, nigga. Anytime you can get a nigga to cum down your throat, is pat yourself on the back worthy. A deal is a deal. However, you are only getting two of the bags."

I watched his eyebrows furrow, yet he remained silent.

So, I continued, "Yes, you sucked my dick and yes, I did cum...however that was most certainly not the best head that I've ever gotten. Quite the opposite. These two bags will still last you a couple of days. When you run out, come and see me. I may have another job lined up for you. Keep practicing and you may get all three bags next time," with that, I squeezed my crotch as I bellowed out a hearty laugh.

Mr. Berry never did respond to my crazy ass. He just snatched his work out of my hand and took off to an isolated corner in the main room.

"It was a pleasure doing business with you Mr. B." I said to get under his skin.

I fell out laughing when that pussy flipped me the bird before turning his back to me. I didn't give a shit though; my nuts were ten pounds lighter thanks to him!

« Chapter 27 It's Trichy »

The Past "Alicia"

I HAD NEVER IN MY life felt this level of sadness before. My mom and Cee Cee were very concerned about me. I had begged my mom to allow me to finish out the remainder of the school year at home. My school allowed it because I had always been a great student. I just could not fathom the thought of facing Mike right now. I wasn't eating or exercising the way that I should've been.

I had actually lost seven pounds according to my last doctor's appointment. My original appointment was scheduled on a Monday. I had rescheduled the day of my ultrasound because I was pretty sure that Mike would show up in an attempt to get me to talk to him. His ass just didn't understand that there would never be any reconciliation between us.

Sure enough when I had called the next day, the receptionist reported that he had come in looking for me. I rescheduled the appointment for Thursday of that same week. A couple of days prior to my appointment, I had noticed that I was experiencing some vaginal itching and an unusual odor. I assumed that it was the beginning of yet another yeast infection.

I had experienced a couple already during this pregnancy. But this time was a little different. First of all, the smell was much more pungent than when I had my other yeast infections. Secondly, I noticed a grayish-yellow, frothy discharge in my panties and also on the tissue when I wiped. Then there was a slight burning sensation when I urinated. It wasn't excruciating, but it stung just enough to grab my attention.

I glanced down at my vagina and said, "Damn bitch, your ass is always doing something! If it's not one thing, then it's another with you!" I scolded my leaky cooch. I swear, pussies could be such nuisances sometimes!

On the day of my ultrasound, my mother and Cee Cee were in attendance of course. As predicted by everyone, I was having a boy. Mike and I had originally planned on making our son a Jr, but fuck Mike! I wish I *would* name my son after his trifling ass. I wasn't even going to give my baby his last name. He just wasn't worthy.

I know some of you are probably thinking that I'm being extra, but fuck you too! He truly deserved a round of applause because he damn sure played his role extremely well. He had me believing everything he said. I never in a million years would've thought that someone else would bear his firstborn child. His scandalous ass had me reevaluating so many things. Even about myself and my lack of judgement.

I had no intentions on dealing with him until after I had our son. I wouldn't dare keep him away from our baby, I just personally wanted no parts or dealings with him. I was not inviting him to the birth either. I wanted to be surrounded by my loved ones on that special day. The sight of him would only make me sick. I had given so much of myself to a guy who was not worthy of receiving even half of me.

When we found out that I was having a baby boy. I couldn't have been happier. I immediately pondered what he'd look like. What would he decide to be as an adult? I could not wait to meet my son. Of course, my mother and Cee Cee gloated and threw out a million, 'I told you so's'. They were right! I waited for Cee Cee and my mother to step out of the room before I told the doctor about my yeast infection. As I described my symptoms she frowned up and told me that she wanted to examine me.

"That does not sound like a yeast infection," She stated.

I was a little annoyed and embarrassed because I wasn't exactly prepared for anyone to look at my pussy. I thought that she was just going to prescribe something for my yeast infection and let me go. In my depressive state, I had neglected to shave downtown, and I didn't want her to smell the scent that I couldn't seem to wash off due to that damn yeast infection.

She placed my feet in the stirrups as she proceeded to perform my pelvic examination. She swabbed me and told me to sit tight while she examined the samples under the microscope. She returned to the examination room approximately thirty minutes later. She had on her poker face.

She began, "Alicia, based on the specimen samples I've collected, you have contracted Trichomoniasis, which is a sexually transmitted infection. You also have bacterial vaginosis which is not an STI. That would explain the strong odor that you mentioned earlier. It is similar to a yeast infection, but it has its distinct differences.

The vagina typically has a pH balance range of about 3.5 to 4.5. We need our vaginas to remain more acidic. Unfortunately, when the pH of your vagina rises above 4.5, it then becomes more alkaline. This leaves the vagina open to an overgrowth of good and bad bacteria within the vagina.

Luckily, both infections can be cleared up with the same antibiotic, Metronidazole. Do not consume any alcohol while taking the antibiotic. Also, eat something before you take the medication, it can make you nauseous. I recommend that you start taking a probiotic daily and eat one to two cups of yogurt a day.

If you are douching, stop. If you are considering having sex with whoever you've contracted the STI from, don't. At least refrain from sex until he is treated as well. Just to air on the side of caution, I'm going to draw your labs and also give you a rapid HIV test while I have you here, okay?"

"That nasty bitch! He actually burned me with his dirty dick having ass! Oh my God!!!" I broke down crying. I sobbed so loud and hard that my entire body shook.

"Will any of this affect my baby, Dr. Green?" I inquired, afraid of her response.

"Alicia, I highly doubt it. You were tested for STIs and HIV just a few months ago during your first prenatal checkup. All of your tests came back negative then. That means you were recently exposed. Luckily, we caught both infections very early and now we are going to treat them.

I'm happy that you've paid attention to your body and was able to identify your abnormal symptoms. Obviously prolonged exposure to any STI can be harmful, especially as it relates to future pregnancies. I assure you that I will do everything that I can to deliver you a healthy baby boy," Dr. Green declared.

"I truly cannot believe that he had the gall to cheat on *me*, have a baby on *me* and now he burned *me*. He is so pathetic!" I tearfully seethed.

Dr. Green had always been my mother's OB-GYN. So, you better believe, she came highly recommended. I loved her outgoing personality. I never felt intimidated around her. She explained things well and ensured that I never left her office with unanswered questions.

I was seeing pure red by the end of our exchange. I got dressed, had my labs drawn and completed my rapid HIV testing. Thankfully the HIV testing came back negative. I know for a fact, I would not have been able to cope with that dreadful diagnosis.

I could kill Mike for this. Literally, kill his black ass! I walked into the waiting area where my mother and best friend were sitting. They both looked at me trying to figure out why I had taken so long and why I had been crying. But I remained silent.

Before we reached the car, my mother gently grabbed my arm and asked, "Alicia is everything okay with the baby? Why are you crying sweetheart?"

"The baby is fine ma. Mike burned me! He gave me some shit called Trickoponamus or some crap like that. Plus, I have some bacterial fishy pussy disease. My pussy is falling apart at the hinges! This just can't be my life right now!!!" I choked out between tears.

My mom and Cee Cee both stared at me before bursting out into a fit of laughter.

"So...my coochie smells like it is rotting from the inside, out and you two are just standing there laughing at me. I swear there's a dead rat hiding in there," I exaggerated before cracking a smile.

Only those two could make me smile after finding out that I had been given an STI.

"Lee Lee I'm sorry baby, but you just screwed Trichomoniasis all the way up!" My mother chuckled.

With my mother being a nurse, she took pronouncing medical terminology seriously. It was her pet peeve.

"But on a serious note, please let this be a lesson to you both. I know you're pissed right now, but you better start thanking God since he spared you from something much worse. Stop relying on those boys to use protection. You, young ladies need to be proactive and protect yourselves.

If you *must* have sex, start bringing your own condoms. You both know that you can come to me about things like this. I'd much rather pay for birth control than for Enfamil, diapers and an antibiotic to treat Trich. Boy do I have a few choice words for that little bastard the next time I see him," She fumed.

"I have never hated anyone in my entire life, but I really hate him. He has taken a love so pure and beautiful and tainted it. I can't believe he put me and our baby at risk like this. This hurts me to the core. Mike never liked wearing condoms, ma. In hindsight, I almost feel that he got me pregnant on purpose. Like this is his sick way of controlling me. "

I had decided in that moment that I had wasted enough tears on that jerk. The three of us went to a nearby Walgreens so that I could pick up my antibiotic and a probiotic.

It was funny how I deliberately didn't invite him to this appointment, yet he still found a way to overshadow the joy of me finding out the sex of my baby. We went to pick up the twins and then headed to one of my favorite places, The Cheesecake Factory.

∞

My mom had changed the phone number to our house after realizing that Mike was not going to obey her request for him to stop calling. He had stopped by the house unannounced several times as well. I'd peek out of one of the windows until he'd finally give up and leave.

With me finishing up this school year at home, it was easy to ignore his ass. I rarely left the house. When I did leave, it was when I knew he was at school, basketball or football practice. I didn't want to hear any of the bullshit lies that he was sure to spew from his deceptive lips.

It had been over four months since I had seen Mike with his baby and the child's mother at the mall. I was now eight months pregnant and was bigger than a house. I couldn't get comfortable. My feet were always swollen, my back constantly ached, and I felt as if my nose were HUGE! On a positive note, my baby had given me even more ass and hips. Plus, my breasts were now fuller than ever.

Through some internal investigations, I had discovered that he and his child's mother had been on and off for years. He had been playing me the entire time. Her name was Tamar and their daughter was now five months old. They had named her Michaela after Mike.

They apparently were not together, although Tamar wanted to be with Mike. I cannot say that these findings didn't make me feel some type of way, because they did. But what was a girl to do? I was not moving backwards. I hoped that he and Tamar were able to remain civil for the sake of their baby.

School was almost out for the summer. I was happy that my due date fell during the summer break. I'd be able to return to school with everyone else in August. Hopefully by then, Mike would have moved on and would focus only on our son and his daughter. Cee Cee had called me frantic a couple of weeks ago because Mike had even resorted to showing up at her house and her job a few times, trying to get to me.

Luckily her parents were not at home either time. I'm sure her parents would have killed her, had they been home. Cee Cee stated that he had begged her to talk to me on his behalf. She quickly dismissed him each time. She had confronted him about the baby and the STI.

He claimed that he was drunk when he had gotten Tamar pregnant. He stated that she had probably poked holes into the condom in order to trap him. He vehemently denied giving me Trich. In fact, he supposedly got pissed off and accused me of messing around on him. He was so pitiful. I only wished that I had seen it all sooner.

He was still excelling in the sports department. Despite our woes, I still wished him the best. Now that I was no longer devastated over our breakup, I had resumed my workouts. I was walking around a nearby track, trying to remain as active as I could. Two miles into my walk, I decided to take a quick break.

I was out of breath and greedily gulping my water. Suddenly someone roughly bumped into me making me spill water down my chin and onto my shirt. I was immediately pissed off. How could anyone not see my big pregnant ass standing here drinking my water?! Then they didn't have the home training to say 'excuse me'.

As I turned around to see who the ass wipe was, I was quickly pushed onto the ground. Lying on my back, I finally got a good look at who was fucking with me. Tamar and a short brown skin girl were standing over me and screaming obscenities.

Tamar furiously pushed me back onto the ground each time I attempted to stand up. She then began to rain blows all over my face and body. My protruding belly was not spared from the vicious attack. I defended myself the best that I could. Had I not been pregnant, she wouldn't have been a match for me.

At eight months pregnant, I was in no condition to fight. My primary concern was protecting my round midsection. The other girl just stood there watching Tamar's attack against me. While she didn't participate in the attack, she did nothing to stop it either. She looked almost remorseful, yet she did nothing to help me or my son. For that, I owed her a generous ass whooping once I delivered my son.

As Tamar continued to rain blows all over my body, I prayed for God to intervene in some way. She was now pulling chunks of my hair out from my scalp. I was in total agony.

After she grew tired, she hocked up a massive loogie and decorated my battered face with it. Then her crazy ass produced a razor from nowhere and proceeded to carve a long slit into my right cheek. I knew that cut would never disappear. She then started unevenly chopping my hair off with the blade. When I looked at her, I only saw pure evil.

She then stated, "Bitch you just couldn't stay away from Mike, could you?! He is my man and I don't give a shit about that bastard inside of you. I bet your skank ass is the one who burned him, causing him to burn me. You nasty hoe. You're the reason why he doesn't want to be with me and my daughter. You're a distraction. You are a scandalous, homewrecking little bitch.

Unfortunately for you, you must be eliminated. I'm sick of competing with your high-saddity ass. It's a wrap for you hoe. I doubt that he'll want you now that I've fucked up your face...but I have to make sure. I refuse to allow you to have my man's son. I'm sorry, but I just can't. Perhaps in another lifetime, you and I could've been friends."

She then snatched the other girl's purse off her shoulder.

"Alicia I'm not into torturing people. Your death will be quick and painless. And so, will his," she stated pointing the gun at my abdomen.

Through my swollen lips, I begged, "Look Tamar, I haven't talked to Mike in over four months. After I found out about you, I left him for good. I don't want anything to do with him anymore. Please just let us go. I'll stay away from him for good. No one has to get hurt. It isn't worth it. Between me and you, this isn't even his baby." I lied, desperate for her to end her relentless attack.

"Bitch do I look stupid to you?! Hey Shay, do you hear this broad over here?" She scoffed to her friend.

She continued, "I know you are still fucking with Mike. He rarely comes home anymore. He hasn't been by to see me or his daughter in two weeks because he has been laying up under your fat ass!" With that she callously kicked me in my stomach.

I doubled over in excruciating pain. I felt terrible for my son. I hadn't felt him move in a while and he was typically very active. Following the kick, I felt a gush of fluid trickling out of my vagina. It was a mixture of amniotic fluid and blood. Fuck! I can't be going into labor now!

"Please! I'm not lying. You need to get me to a hospital! My water just broke. I promise that I haven't seen Mike in months. Please don't do this!"

Ignoring me she replied, "I'm sorry, but it's already done. Rest in hell, bitch!!!" She screamed as I felt hot lead pierce through my stomach, followed by another bullet being lodged into my chest.

To Be Continued

My Brother's Lady, My Baby 1

Available Now!!!

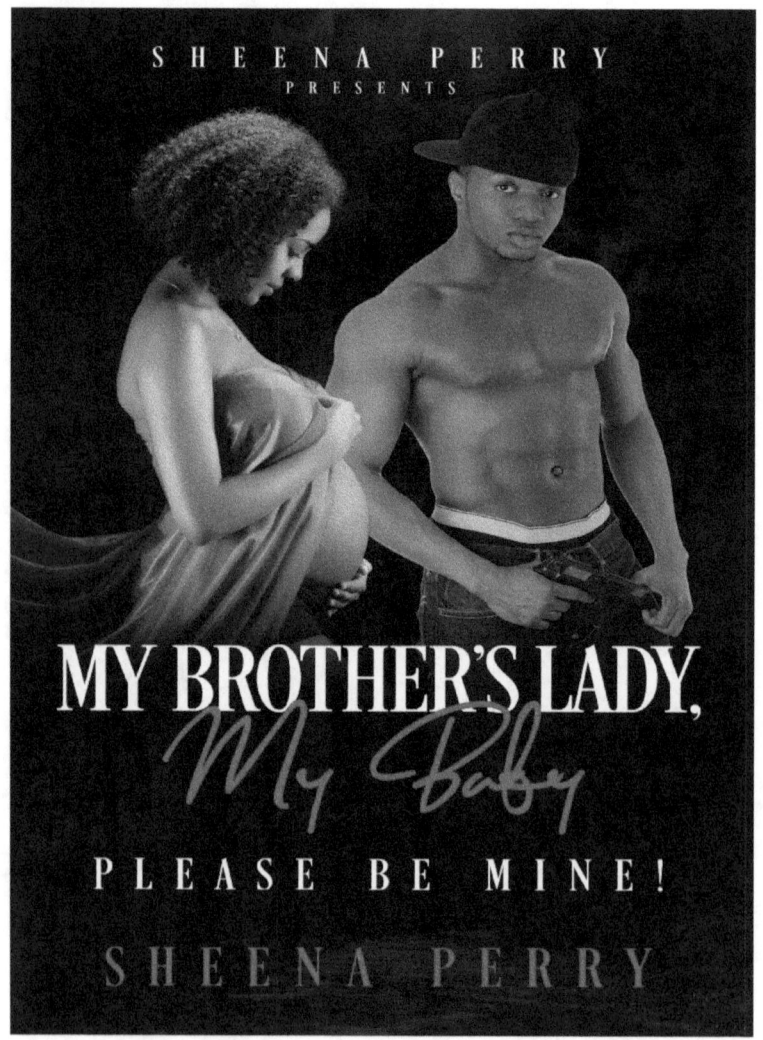

Inevitable Deceptions: A Heart's Journey to Nowhere 2

Available Now!!!

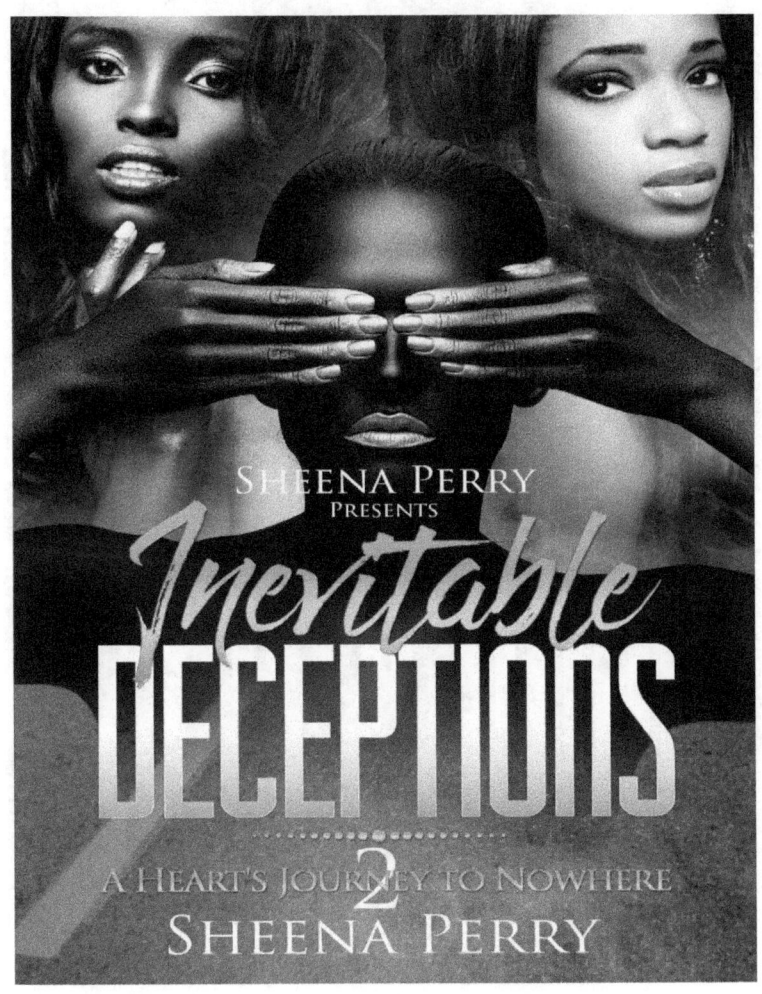

My Wife's Daughters

Available Now!!!

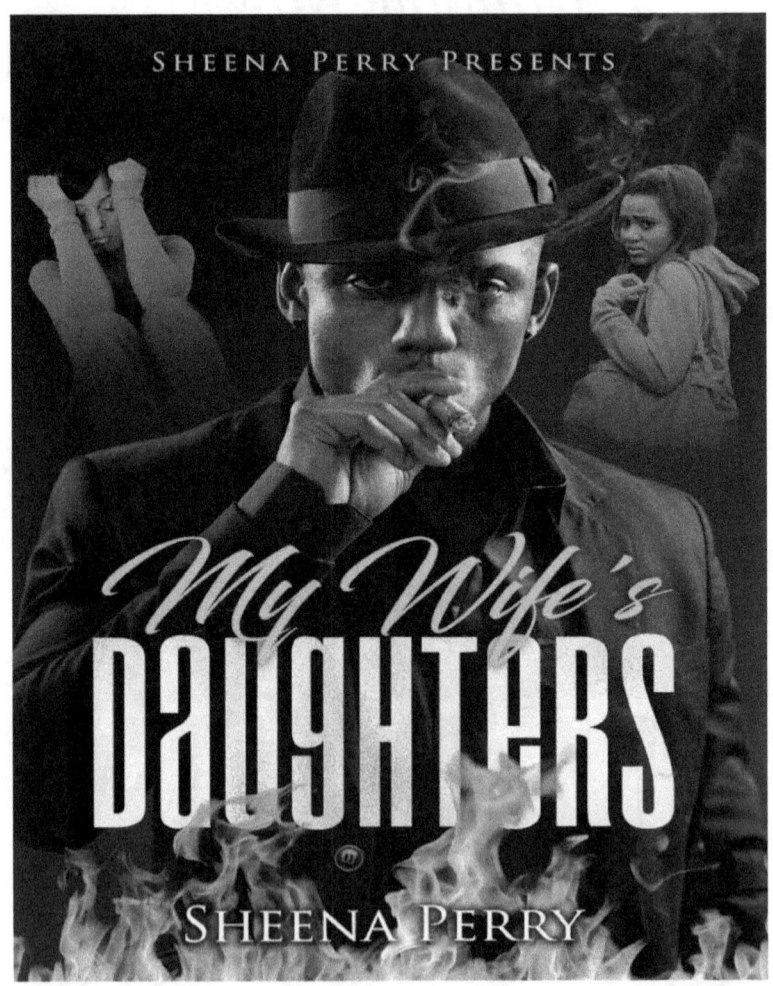

They Call Me Junior: A Gay Love Story

Available Now!!!

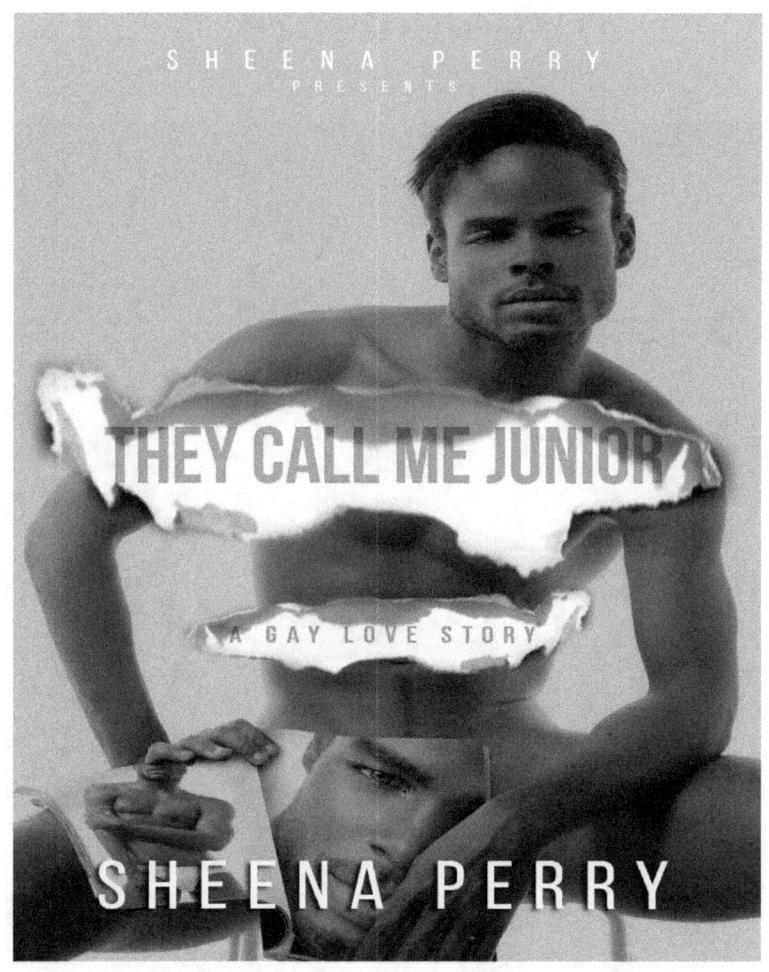

Releases From Other Authors

Available Now!!!

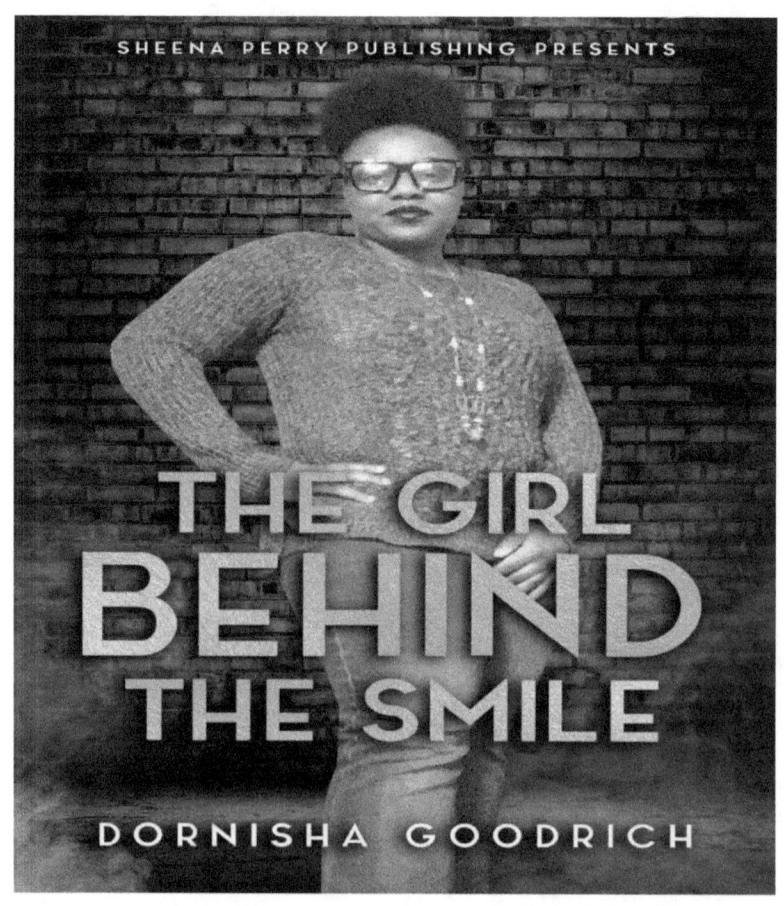

Releases From Other Authors

Available Now!!!